# RACER

IRON ROGUES MC

FIONA DAVENPORT

# RACER

Jude "Racer" Iverson's mission was simple: identify who was rigging cars and causing dangerous crashes on the underground racing circuit. But then he fell hard and fast for the pretty mechanic who wanted answers about the wreck that put her brother in a coma.

When the threats turned deadly, Racer vowed to protect Emily Novak at all costs. Even if it meant breaking every rule in the book.

# PROLOGUE

The steady beeping was good under these circumstances. But I hated what the sound represented.

It wasn't supposed to be like this. My brother was supposed to be yelling at someone to swap out the damn tires faster or laughing with the guys after a win. Not lying motionless in a hospital bed with a machine breathing for him.

I sat on the edge of my chair at his bedside, one hand curled around his, the other gripping the sleeve of my hoodie. Staring at his face, I searched for a sign that he was going to wake up. An eyelid twitch, a muscle flinch, anything.

Aside from the bruise on his jaw and the split lip, he looked like he was just sleeping. Except

Mason usually would've opened his eyes the second I stepped into the room. His situational awareness was off the charts, which was one of the things that made him so damn good behind the wheel.

"They keep saying it was driver error," I whispered, squeezing his hand. "But I know better. They're wrong."

My brother didn't react.

"Nobody believes me. Not the doctors. Not even the crew." It had taken a lot of hard work, sweat, and time to earn the respect of the pit crew and other mechanics. So I'd been even more disappointed when they brushed off my suspicions. "They think I'm just upset over what happened to you and refusing to accept reality." My voice broke as tears streamed down my cheeks. "But something was wrong with your ride. I felt it in my bones before you even took the first turn."

And I had the sinking feeling he knew it, too. The way he went quiet on the radio. How his voice sounded tighter than usual. Not scared, exactly. Just off.

I should've said something. Stopped him from racing. Gotten him out of that car.

A soft knock pulled me from the spiral I'd been

circling since Mason crashed into the wall on that sharp turn.

Kane stepped inside, his footsteps quiet and heavy as the door shut behind him.

He looked at my brother first. A long, quiet stare with his jaw so tight I thought it might crack.

Then his gaze slid to me. "Emily."

Letting go of my brother's hand, I stood. "Hey, Kane."

He crossed the room in two long strides and pulled me into a brief hug, one arm wrapped tight across my shoulders, the other braced around the back of my head as though he could shield me from everything. I buried my face in his cut and tried not to completely fall apart.

"Are you okay?" I asked although it seemed like a dumb question, considering the circumstances.

His brows drew together as he shook his head. "Fuck, no. I just feel like I let you both down."

My shoulders slumped. "I understand better than you know."

After guiding me back to the chair, Kane jerked his chin at Mason. "I might be his club president, but we both know your brother would have my ass for making you feel worse."

"You didn't." I heaved a deep sigh. "Not really."

"Quit beating yourself up. This isn't your fault," he reassured me, grabbing the other chair so he could sit on the other side of Mason's bed.

I shot him a guilty look. "I'm his mechanic, and his car failed."

"Assistant mechanic. But even if you weren't, the buck doesn't stop with you."

I quirked my brow, and he added, "Yeah, I get that you do a hell of a lot more than most in your spot because Axle trusts you with his ride. But there's shit going down you don't know about. So it bears repeating...this is not your fault."

Squeezing my eyes shut, I took a deep breath and let his certainty ease some of my guilt. It helped. A little.

When Kane formed the Redline Kings MC and my brother decided to prospect, he'd warned me there would be things he couldn't share. So I knew better than to demand an explanation since it sounded like Mason's wreck was related to club business.

Opening my eyes again to meet Kane's unflinching gaze, I asked. "Is there anything I can do to help?"

"You said something to the crew just after the

crash. Before you hopped into the ambulance with Axle."

"I did." I crossed my arms over my chest, suddenly cold. "Fat lot of good that did me."

"Then tell me. I'm listening."

"I think something was off." My throat burned. "Which doesn't make any sense. I went over every inch of that car before I went to bed the night before the race. But I heard the way it hit when he zoomed past me on the last lap. Next thing I knew, he was spinning out like he had no control of the car, then he slammed into the barrier. They're saying it was bad shift timing or oversteering."

The silence stretched, thick with my rage over what happened to Mason.

Kane finally said, "You think someone tampered with it."

"I know it sounds far-fetched, but I can't come up with another explanation." My eyes burned. "He wouldn't have made a mistake like that. Not in a million years."

"I believe you."

That stopped me cold. All I could do was blink before I mumbled, "You...what?"

"Can't give you a hell of a lot right now, but there've been other crashes recently that caught my attention. Didn't know those drivers very well, though. Axle's wreck erased any doubts I had. Something's going on. Not sure what yet."

A hollow relief fluttered in my chest. As much as knowing that Kane believed I wasn't responsible for the crash helped, my brother was still in a coma.

"I know Axle is all the blood family you have left, but you're not alone in this. I will always have your back and his. So will the rest of the club."

"Let me help you find out who did this," I pleaded. "I know what to look for."

"No."

The single word hit me hard.

"You're not getting dragged into this any deeper. Your brother would fucking shoot me if I let anything happen to you."

"You better hope he wakes up and tries," I muttered.

"Emily."

"No," I snapped, tears prickling my eyes. "He's all I have, Kane. Someone tried to erase him. And ruin his name while they were at it. I can't just sit back and let that happen."

"I get where you're coming from, but you have my word they're not gonna get away with this," he vowed, his eyes filled with determination. "I need you to stay out of it, though."

I dropped my gaze and nodded. "Okay. But can I at least take a look at his car?"

Kane hesitated, then nodded, filling me with relief. He didn't say anything else. Just got to his feet, rounded the bed, gave my shoulder one last squeeze, then looked at my brother one more time and left.

After the door clicked shut behind him, I picked up Mason's hand again and squeezed.

"I lied," I whispered. "I'm not staying out of it."

My voice shook, but the promise didn't.

"I'm going to find who did this to you. I'm going to clear your name, no matter what it takes."

# 1

---

RACER

The air inside the garage attached to the Iron Rogues MC's clubhouse was thick and warm. April in Old Bridge, Tennessee, was always unpredictable, but I didn't mind. Other than when I was on the track, this was my favorite space—me, my bike, and the hum of steel under pressure.

I had my head buried under the frame of my old '79 Triumph Bonneville, one arm jammed up against the manifold, the other balancing a wrench as I adjusted the throttle body. Sweat trickled down my spine, and there was a streak of grease across my cheek from where I'd scratched an itch without thinking.

The bike was a piece of art, rough and unforgiving—like most of the brothers who called this club family.

I was elbow deep in my machine for another twenty minutes before I was ready to start her up. I slid out from under the frame and stood, wiping my hands on a rag before bringing her to life. The roar of my baby's engine purred through the garage like a satisfied growl. The chrome gleamed in the rays of morning sunlight coming through the high windows. She was streaked with just enough grit to remind me she'd been run hard and put away even harder.

I gave the throttle another little twist and listened to her purr.

"That's it, girl," I muttered, wiping sweat from my brow with the back of my arm. "You're ready to eat pavement and spit out flames."

My phone buzzed on the workbench. I didn't even glance at the screen. There weren't many people who would bother calling me this early unless it was club shit.

"Yeah?" I answered.

"My office. Now," Fox grunted, then hung up.

I immediately shut off my bike, then tossed the rag into a laundry bin before walking to the sink. My black tee stuck to my back from the heat, and my jeans were smeared with grime. But I didn't even consider going to my room to shower and change first.

When the president summoned, you fucking went. Especially when the man in question was Kye "Fox" Pearson—part CEO, part mercenary, full-time hard-ass. Didn't matter if you were bleeding out or balls deep in your old lady. Fox didn't call unless it mattered.

I washed my hands quickly, swiped the grease off my face, then grabbed my cut off the hook by the door, slung it over my shoulders, and headed inside. I walked by Ice as I crossed through the kitchen, who raised a brow as I passed.

"Heard Fox needed to see you. Someone finally caught your internet search history?" he asked, grinning.

His old lady, Marnie, giggled from the chair beside him, making the one-year-old little girl on her lap babble happily.

"Only thing I google is torque specs and how to steal your wife," I shot back, flipping him off over my shoulder.

A loud growl and shout of female laughter trailed me.

I pushed the door open without knocking—Fox never expected us to—and stepped into the room.

Fox's office was like him—clean, controlled, and intimidating. The place was spotless, built like a fucking exec's war room with a massive desk, chairs clean enough to perform surgery on, and a big round conference table where we hashed out plans that weren't always legal.

On the far wall was a bar and a lounge area with a couple of chairs and battered sofas. There was also a side door that led to Maverick's office, which was a similar setup, but the decor made the differences in personality between the president and the VP very clear. Still, the two were best friends and worked seamlessly as a team to lead the Iron Rogues. There wasn't a single patch who didn't respect the hell out of them and trust them with our lives.

Fox stood near the desk, arms crossed over his chest, that signature scowl carved into his face as though he'd been born with it there. Salt-and-pepper scruff on his jaw, tattoos curling down his arms, and a fucking stare—sharp brown eyes, strategic and calculating—that could cut through a man's soul and sort the guilty from the stupid.

Maverick stood near the door to his adjoining office, sipping black coffee and radiating quiet menace. Although to most, he would appear casual and relaxed, with a typical smirk on his lips as he shoved his dark auburn hair away from his face.

Storm sat on one of the old couches, arms crossed, tattoos coiling down his biceps. His legs were spread, elbows on his knees, and concerned, dark eyes trained on Kane.

I hadn't noticed the visitor at first. He leaned against the edge of the conference table, dressed similarly to the rest of us. A plain tee, jeans, and a leather cut, except his vest told the world he was the president of the Redline Kings Motorcycle Club. His sharp gaze and lethal edge belied the easy smile he threw my way.

Kane had been a close ally to the Iron Rogues ever since Storm had been a prospect. He'd helped us on numerous occasions, and we'd done the same for him. He'd earned my respect and trust over and over. Though he wasn't patched into our club, he was family.

"Thought maybe you finally choked on a carburetor," Maverick said dryly, arching a brow.

"Fuck you, I was elbow deep in my girl," I muttered. "And she's got better curves than any of you assholes."

A smirk stretched across Kane's face, and he

drawled, "Was startin' to think you'd wrecked that pretty bike of yours."

I snorted. "If I wreck, it's intentional. Just more dramatic that way."

Kane chuckled, sharp and dry. "Good. I need dramatic."

Fox rolled his eyes. "Sit your ass down, Racer."

I dropped onto the chair across from him, sprawled out, and put one boot up on the edge of the table just to annoy him. He shot me a look, and I grinned.

"Take your fucking boot off my desk, Racer," Fox said, voice cool as frost, "or I'll cut it off at the ankle and nail the damn thing to the wall as a warning."

I chuckled but slid my foot down. Not because I thought he was serious—mostly. With Fox, you could never be completely sure.

Kane's easy smile faded. "Shit's fucked in Florida. Got something that needs your particular skill set."

I raised an eyebrow. "Which one? My charming personality?"

Maverick snorted at that, and I frowned in mock offense.

"My talent with a stick?"

Storm shook his head, muttering, "Considering your monk-like existence lately, having a hard time believing you've got any skill with a stick off the track."

I shrugged, skipping over the monk comment. It had been a long fucking time since my dick had even twitched for a woman.

"I'd prove it," I drawled, "but I'm not about to give some chick a reason to think I'm next on the list just to show off my prowess."

"Next on the list?" Kane asked.

"To fall for his woman," Maverick explained with a smirk. "Racer's under the bullshit impression that he's stronger than the rest of us. Thinks he can't be tamed by a woman."

Rolling my eyes, I rested one foot on my opposite knee. "You call me in here to play matchmaker?"

It was Kane who snorted this time. "Not my type, Racer, but I'm flattered."

"Your loss," I quipped.

Even Fox cracked a smile at that before his expression became stoic again and he got back to business. "Kane's got a problem. One that might be bigger than it looks on the surface."

I looked at Kane, who was all serious now.

"This about the Redline crash?" I queried. "Saw the footage."

The Redline Kings MC was at the center of a racing empire—both legal and underground. One ruled by Kane.

He was a fucking legend on the track, but it wasn't his wall of trophies that kept him at the top. Though he didn't look it, he was a brilliant businessman, a fucking billionaire. And someone no one dared to fuck with.

He was known for his sharp reflexes, calm dominance, and operating with brutal precision. He valued loyalty and had a reputation for being merciless to those who crossed him—especially when it came to protecting the integrity of his races.

Recently, one of his drivers had clipped the turn and drove straight into a support beam, causing the pit-side building to collapse. It had nearly killed the driver and three people inside.

Kane nodded, leaning forward slightly, and bracing his hands on his thighs.

"Thank fuck for Wrecker," he murmured. "That motherfucker reads debris like a blueprint."

Wrecker was one of my club brothers. A civil engineer who was trained to safely dismantle or clear debris from disaster sites to facilitate rescue efforts.

There wasn't anyone better, and through cameras, he'd been able to talk them through the rubble to get to the trapped people and get them out.

"Thing is," Kane said, his voice cool and eyes hard, "underground circuit's been getting hit hard. That's not the only wreck."

I frowned. "Meaning?"

"Meaning I've had six drivers crash in the past few months. And a handful more from other teams. Wrecks on the underground circuit are fucking piling up. Most walked away, but a couple didn't. Two fatalities—both when the cars caught fire before we could get them out in time." He exhaled slowly, as though he was trying not to snap. "They've all been blamed on driver error, but I know my fucking crew. Something's off."

My jaw ticked. "You think someone's fucking with the cars?"

"I think someone's fucking with the entire circuit," Kane confirmed.

Something in his voice darkened. Kane was cold steel when he needed to be, but I knew those deaths had to weigh on him. He ran a tight domain, one where skill and loyalty meant everything.

"Then a few days ago, my Road Captain, Axle, went down," Kane continued. "Took a turn sharp, car didn't respond. He's in a coma now. Might not wake up. His sister's..." He paused, jaw tightening. "She's the only family he's got."

"Besides you," Storm added.

Kane's expression broke for just a second, just long enough for me to see the pain behind his controlled exterior.

"Kid's been with me since before the patch. I straddled my time between here and my hometown growing up. Knew him and his sister since I was sixteen. He helped me build my first garage when I was scrappin' parts in a shed. All Axle wanted was to be out on the track. And damn," Kane chuckled, "fucker used to race circles around me in his sleep. His accident—" Kane broke off, his expression turning cold and deadly. He pushed away from the desk and planted his feet wide, crossing his arms over his chest. "I promised his sister I'd find out what the fuck's happening."

"He thinks it's tied to betting," Storm tossed out.

I looked at Kane, my head tilting. "Throwing races?"

"Yeah," he answered. "I started noticing patterns in the bets. The losses line up too clean with spikes in betting shifts. Payouts swing hard right before a wreck. Either drivers are being paid to throw races, or someone's making sure they don't finish. My tech guy's been watching it, but then the crashes started. Either someone's covering fuckups...or they're escalating."

Storm's voice was sharp as a knife. "You think it's sabotage?"

"I do," Kane replied. "And not random. It's clean. Precise. You don't see it until it's too fuckin' late. I have helmet cams on my drivers now and surveillance at the big tracks. Still, whoever it is slips in and out without a trace."

Fox looked at me, finally speaking. "Kane wants to borrow you."

My brow lifted. "Borrow me? You sure you're ready for the responsibility?"

Storm muttered, "Only reason he's letting you go is 'cause Fox doesn't want you wrecking too much shit around here without supervision."

"Fuck all of you," I said cheerfully. "You know I drive better than any asshole on wheels."

"You're not just racing," Fox warned. "You're drawing them out. Letting them think they have a new mark. Then we burn them down."

I grinned. "I get to play bait? Sounds fun."

Kane nodded. "You have the skills and the name. You've got a reputation in both worlds—legal and underground. People remember you. You showing up on the circuit will draw attention. Whoever's fucking with my races won't be able to resist taking a swing at you. That's what I want."

I glanced around the room, at my brothers. Every one of them had risked their lives for me at one point or another. That included Kane. And I'd do the same in a heartbeat.

"I'm in."

Maverick chuckled low. "You're seriously not gonna ask for details first?"

"Nah." I shrugged. "I trust Kane. Besides, I've been itching for a good run. And if I get to break someone's nose along the way? Even better."

Fox's brow arched, dry as sandpaper. "Try not to wreck too much without backup."

I smirked. "You saying I'm not allowed to have fun?"

"I'm saying if you end up face-down in a ditch with your spine bent sideways, I'll be pissed I wasted the manpower hauling your cocky ass home."

"No promises." I pushed to my feet. "But I'll make sure to at least get it on camera when I go up in flames."

Storm snorted. "You wreck, you better make sure

it's on fucking purpose. Otherwise, we're gonna start calling you Pancake."

"Fuck off," I said, flashing them a grin.

Kane extended a hand, and I took it, the grip firm, mutual respect locked between us.

"When do you want me down there?"

"Three days. That'll give me time to set the roster and brief my crew. I'll send the address for the compound in Florida," Kane said. "You'll crash at our clubhouse. My VP, Edge, will get you up to speed on the track and the drivers. You'll meet the crew, inspect the vehicles, and begin practicing. One of mine's gonna drop out with an injury. You'll take his place. Then you'll race. You win a few, even if you lose a few, it'll start making waves. If they're watching the standings—and they are—you'll catch their eye and flush the fucker out."

"If all doesn't go well?" I asked, curious if he had a backup plan.

Kane's smile sharpened. "Then we do what we always do. Handle it."

"Works for me." I stood and looked at Fox, who gave me a nod.

Storm slapped my back as I passed. "Just don't fuckin' die. We don't have enough patience to train a new you."

"And the world can barely handle one of me," I said, smirking.

Fox's voice followed me as I reached the door. "Racer."

I paused.

Fox stepped around the desk, folding his arms across his chest as he stared me down. "Don't fuck around on this. Find whoever's doing this and make sure they regret breathing."

I grinned, teeth bared. "I'll make sure they bleed out slow enough to regret every bad decision they ever made."

Storm's mouth twitched. "Try not to get brain matter on your boots. Shit's hard to scrub out."

Kane clapped me on the shoulder. "You're gonna like my team. They're as tight as the Iron Rogues, and they don't fuck around."

"Let me guess," I said, slinging my cut back over my shoulder. "You got a pit crew full of old mobsters and retired street racers?"

"Close," he said. "But better. One of my best mechanics is about half your size, and she'll probably outsmart your ass before you even finish a sentence."

I snorted. "She hot?"

Kane's expression cooled a little, protective. "She's also Axle's little sister."

That perked my interest in ways I didn't expect. "Good to know."

Maverick shook his head as I headed for the door. "Try not to fall in love, dumbass."

"Don't worry," I called back. "I'm way too smart for that shit."

## 2

---

### EMILY

It was good to be surrounded by cars again, even if the nurses practically had to force me out of the hospital. I'd finally agreed when Kane sent over a Redline Kings prospect who'd taken my spot at his bedside and promised to call if Mason woke up while I was gone.

The garage was quieter than usual. A couple of guys were wrenching on their bikes in the back corner, music low and conversation even lower. Nobody said anything to me as I passed through the main bay, which was exactly how I liked it today.

Mason's car sat near the back—what was left of it. The front end was crushed like an aluminum can, the passenger side mangled beyond repair. But I wasn't looking for cosmetic damage.

I knelt beside the frame, dragging my fingers along the steering wheel. The data logger housing mounted in the middle had been ruined in the crash. When I cracked the casing open, my stomach sank. The device wasn't just corrupted—some of the components were mangled beyond recognition. A high-speed hit straight to that side of the car would've done it.

"Crap," I muttered, sitting back on my heels.

"You sure didn't waste any time takin' a look at Axle's car."

I looked up to see Kane smirking at me from a few feet away.

"Maybe she'll answer me before any of you guys do," I muttered, holding up the mangled logger.

He stepped closer and gave a low whistle. "That's what's left of the data unit?"

"Yeah." I turned it in my hand. "Probably didn't survive the impact."

Kane squinted down at the logger. "No salvaging anything off that."

I nodded slowly, a pit forming in my stomach. "Which means we have no data."

He hesitated. "And no way to prove Axle didn't fuck up and cause the crash."

*Exactly.*

I swallowed hard, setting the shattered unit down. "Mason didn't make that mistake."

"I know." Kane's voice was quiet now. "And so do his club brothers. Anyone else who says otherwise can go fuck themselves."

Standing, I wiped my palms on my jeans. "If it'd been anywhere else, he'd be facing sanctions."

Kane clapped me on the back. "Then it's a damn good thing I own the underground races in the entire state, because nobody is gonna keep Axle off the track when he finally wakes the fuck up."

I appreciated his use of when instead of if. Mason had been in a coma for nearly a week, and it was getting harder by the day to remain positive.

Snorting, I mumbled, "I'd like to see them try."

Kane shook his head with a chuckle. "Not sure who's more stubborn, you or your brother."

"It definitely runs in the family."

I had pestered Kane to give me the chance to show him what I could do under the hood of one of his race cars. When I was only fifteen, he finally caved, handed me a lug wrench, and pointed at the rear tire of the nearest car, telling me to change it as fast as I could. Since I grew up trailing my big brother, and he spent all his time either in the garage or on a track, it wasn't much of a challenge. But it took me a while to realize Kane knew that since my brother hadn't kept any secrets from him. Which meant he was well aware that Mason had let me do more than hand him tools when he was working on cars for years before then.

Grabbing a nearby racing jack, I had the vehicle off the ground in seconds. Then I swapped out the wrench for a hydraulic wheel gun. The entire wheel assembly was off and replaced in under a minute. When it was done, I dusted my hands off and grinned at Kane.

He'd hired me on the spot and had given me the experience I needed to earn my ASE certification. That first week had been brutal. Every guy in the garage watched me as though they were waiting for me to break something. Or cry. Just because I was a girl. *Jerks.*

So I worked harder. Faster. Cleaner. I stayed late, got greasy, and kept my mouth shut until I had something worth saying.

Eventually, I earned my spot with them. They didn't treat me like Kane's pet project or Axle's little sister anymore. I was just one of the crew, which was exactly how I wanted it.

"Damn straight, it does," Kane agreed, pulling me out of my memories. "Which is how I know he's gonna be hell on wheels when he wakes up from his coma."

"Yeah," I whispered.

"Hey, Novak!" Gauge called from under a lifted Mustang, his voice muffled. "You skipping the race tomorrow night to hold Axle's hand or what?"

I snorted. "I miss a couple of races 'cause my brother's in a coma, and suddenly the world's ending?"

"That's because you're the only one who double-checks my torque settings," he shot back. "I don't trust any of these other assholes."

"You shouldn't," someone muttered from across the bay.

A few chuckles rippled through the garage, and I rolled my eyes as I wiped off my hands. "I'll be there."

---

THE PIT BUZZED with controlled chaos—shouted instructions, the hiss of pneumatics, the sharp scent of exhaust and burnt rubber. Floodlights cast everything in stark relief, shadows cutting across the concrete.

I moved between cars, barking for a 15mm

socket before the driver even finished complaining, my voice rising over the rumble of engines and the shriek of tires. One of the guys tossed the tool to me without looking.

My hands worked fast, focused, and steady. I was in my element, right where I belonged.

But I still felt the tension lingering under the surface. A few of the guys seemed quieter, and not just when I was nearby, so I didn't think it was because they didn't know how to treat me with Mason in a coma. Some glanced over their shoulders more than usual.

The crew was off tonight. Not in any way that would tank a race, but in the little things. A distracted look here and a too long pause there. My brother's absence felt like an unspoken echo in every motion.

"You feel it too, right?" Piston muttered, dropping beside me as we adjusted a suspension component. "Shit's been off."

I didn't answer except for a sharp nod. I couldn't, not when my chest was already tight from holding it together all night.

Luckily, he didn't push.

Later, while swapping out brake pads, I heard Gauge call over to another crew member. "Kane's bringing in someone new. Some hotshot racer from Tennessee."

I froze. Just for a second. Long enough for the wrench in my hand to slip, nicking my knuckle.

I should have known there would be a new racer to replace my brother. Kane needed to keep things running. There were races to win.

But it still felt like being punched in the chest.

Mason wasn't even awake yet, and someone was already slipping into his shadow while people outside our circle were saying he'd caused the crash.

It pissed me off, but I didn't say anything. Just tightened the bolt and kept working.

I finished up the last brake bleed and handed the tools off to Piston, wiping my hands on a rag as I stepped away from the car.

Engines still roared in the background. From the edge of the pit, I could see the finish line, a blur of heat waves and smoke where tires had eaten up the road.

The crowd screamed as the lead driver crossed, but the noise barely registered.

I was too wrapped up in the hole my brother left behind to really care who won.

The space Mason should've filled was still

empty...and someone else would be standing in it soon.

I didn't know anything about the guy Kane was bringing in except the gossip I'd heard the crew toss around tonight. Some Tennessee racer with a reputation that was bound to make him cocky. Guys like that always acted as if the track owed them something.

But I didn't care how fast he was or how many wins he had.

I didn't need a replacement.

I needed answers.

I tossed the rag onto the workbench and turned away from the track, jaw tight with purpose.

Let Kane's golden boy show up and draw all the attention he wanted.

I was going to figure out what happened to my brother—even if I had to do it all by myself.

## 3

---

### RACER

The Redline Kings' compound was located in a small beach town in Florida called Cross-bend, around twenty minutes south of Tallahassee. Like the Iron Rogues, they pretty much owned the whole town and controlled the surrounding areas, especially if they had raceways located there. Up in Tallahassee, Kane owned Redline Speedway, one of the biggest raceways in the state.

He'd also bought or built several smaller ones throughout Florida to host other races. The tracks for the illegal races were mostly old, abandoned properties he converted. He didn't like street racing because they drew more attention from the cops and were more likely to injure spectators.

Their garage sat a few miles off the main drag,

tucked into the back end of a repurposed industrial block that looked like it'd seen more illegal deals and burnout streaks than OSHA inspections. Chain-link fences, razor wire, sun-bleached asphalt baking under the Florida sun. The air reeked of gasoline, exhaust, motor oil, and the faint tinge of smoke from cigarettes or cigars.

My kind of place. I felt right at home.

I rolled in on my Harley, the familiar rumble of the engine purring beneath me. A couple of the guys working outside straightened up when they saw me coming. Both wore a Redline Kings cut. One nudged the other and said something I didn't catch, but I recognized the posture. Curiosity. Recognition. Anticipation. I'd been racing long enough—both legally and underground—to know when people were itching to see what I could do.

I parked near the front entrance, cut the engine, and slung my leg over the seat, rolling my shoulders out as I walked toward the bay. It had been a long, almost seven-hour ride down here from Old Bridge. Normally, I would enjoy a ride like that, but the heat and humidity—even in April—was oppressive. Next time, I'd have to do it at night when it was cooler.

Heat shimmered off the pavement, the afternoon sun beating down hard, and my boots crunched over grit and loose bolts. A few Redline Kings were leaning near the entrance, watching me as though they were trying to decide whether I was friend or prey. One of them grinned.

"Look what the fuckin' wind blew in," a voice called out from inside, causing a grin to stretch wide across my face.

Edge.

Kane's younger brother and the Redline Kings' VP. Same lethal bloodline, just wired a little differently. The man had a smile like a movie star and eyes that belonged to a damn psycho. When we met, I liked him immediately. Even if he sometimes seemed a little unhinged.

"Been a while, Edge," I said, clasping his forearm when he approached.

"Still smell like burnt rubber and bad decisions," he shot back, slapping my shoulder before we pulled apart.

"Only on my good days," I replied with a smirk.

"Then today must be a fuckin' banner day." He waved me in. "C'mon. Kane's waiting. We got you set up in the clubhouse, but we'll head over there after we show you your office and private bay and get you acquainted with the place."

Inside, the place was a mechanical wet dream—

rows of lifted hoods, scattered tires, tool chests, and racks of parts. Half-dismantled race cars gleamed under fluorescent lights. There were grease stains on the floor, shelves of tools that I was itching to play with, and the distant thrum of an impact wrench buzzing somewhere in the back.

My boots echoed on the concrete as I followed Edge through the chaos. We passed a few mechanics who gave me curious glances, a couple nodding in recognition.

Edge led me down a side hall and into an empty office. Bare bones but functional. The AC worked, it looked clean, and there was a stocked mini fridge. That was all I needed.

Kane was already there, leaning against the counter with a beer in hand.

"How was the ride?"

"Hot as fuck," I replied, dropping my duffel on the ground. "How do you assholes survive breathing bathwater?"

Kane chuckled and cocked his head toward a large picture window on the opposite side of the room. It looked out over a large mechanic bay that was separated from the large area we'd walked through when Edge brought me inside. There was a door next to the window that I assumed led out to the space.

It was large enough to work on both my car and my bike, with plenty of room to spare. On one end, there were shelves stocked with everything I needed to keep my vehicles running perfectly. The opposite wall was a large steel roll-up door. And directly across from the window was a station for cleaning.

"I could get used to a space like that," I murmured.

Edge grinned. "Right? It's also the perfect setup for...private company and after-hours conversations. That's why we have a few rooms like this, located two stories down. Floors are easier to rinse down there." His smile went sharp. "In case anyone gets... difficult. Some folks don't know when to shut up."

Kane rolled his eyes, then looked back at me. "The car you'll be racing will be delivered to the track early tomorrow morning. I have a backup you can use to practice. I haven't reported the substitution yet, though. And I want to keep everything under wraps until the qualifier, so we'll take you out to learn the track after dark."

I nodded. Back in Old Bridge, Kane hadn't mentioned that the race tomorrow night was a qualifier. When I realized it, I brought it up to him. He said he'd have one of his other guys race so I wouldn't have to go in blind. Fuck that. I'd bested plenty of racetracks without even seeing them before I rode my bike or car to the starting line. But to keep him from treating me like a fucking pussy, I showed up this afternoon so I could get some practice before the race.

"Leave your shit here for now," Edge instructed. "I'm heading back to the compound in twenty minutes. I'll take it with me."

"Thanks."

"The boys know why you're here," Kane informed me. "My patches are solid. But I have other employees—drivers, sponsors, freelance techs—who don't wear the cut. Can't guarantee none of 'em are dirty."

I met his eyes. "I'll watch my back."

"We'll do the same," Edge promised.

Kane took a swig from his bottle, then set it down with a soft clink. "The Helline Circuit final's in three weeks. Since it's one of the biggest underground races in the South, and money pours in from half the country, that's most likely when the kingpin behind this shit's gonna make his biggest move."

"You think he'll show his hand?"

"He has to. The kind of payout tied to that race...

it's too big not to. If we don't flush him before then, that's our shot."

I nodded once. "So I put on a show."

Kane's grin sharpened. "Exactly."

He took me through the garage, introducing me as his newest team member. I watched reactions closely but didn't pick up on anything that set off alarm bells.

When the time came, Kane grabbed his keys, and we took his car out to a converted shipping-yard-turned-black-market racetrack.

"Perk of bein' the owner," he grunted as he unlocked the gates and opened them, allowing me to drive right onto the asphalt ring.

I ran laps for a couple of hours, until Kane seemed satisfied. "Now you'll be familiar with the track, and nothing will trip you up on the race."

Stopping in my tracks, I crossed my arms over my chest and turned to face him, scowling. "You treat all your drivers like toddlers?"

"I need you at your best, Racer. Winning is how we get this guy," he snapped.

"You want me to win, I'm gonna do it my way." He opened his mouth, but I held up a hand and added, "The wall of awards and millions in victory cash sitting in my bank are gonna disagree with whatever shit you're about to spew. You came to me, Kane. You can't ask for my help and then put fucking shackles on me. Now, stop helicoptering and let me get shit done."

Kane tossed his head back and laughed heartily.

"Backing off." He held his hands up like he was surrendering. "But if you get hurt, don't expect me to stand between you and Fox."

---

THE NEXT NIGHT, the first underground qualifier roared to life. The course was narrow, gritty, and fast. Just the way I liked it. Oil-streaked pavement, barrels used as fake barriers, crowds pressing in behind chain-link fences and half-assed barricades. Smoke, screams, engine revs—it was beautiful fucking chaos.

I lined up against five other cars, each one idling low. My ride for the night was a midnight-black '72 Chevelle SS that Kane had tuned himself. The bitch purred like a dream and roared like a monster. She had torque, bite, and zero forgiveness. She was fucking perfect.

The race itself was over in less than eight minutes, but I made every second count. From the moment the signal dropped, I hit the gas and slid through the first turn sideways just to make an impression. I played a little dirty—cut off a tailing Nissan at the apex, kicked up grit from the shoulder, and fishtailed right before the final straight just to show I could. Then I floored it, crossing the line a full four seconds ahead of the pack.

The crowd went fucking nuts. Cameras were on me. Whispers flew. And my name started echoing through the pits again.

It was exactly what we wanted.

Keep 'em talking. Let the bastard behind the sabotage watch me and think I was just another cocky asshole with a death wish. That was the bait.

I climbed out of the car, rolled my shoulders, and tugged my gloves off as I headed back toward the garage pit—my adrenaline still singing, the heat of the engine clinging to my skin.

Then I saw her.

And I swear the fucking world tilted.

She stood near one of the workbenches, half turned toward a guy rattling off specs. But I didn't hear a single word. My eyes were glued to her.

She wore a pair of navy-blue mechanic coveralls rolled up to the elbows, the zipper down just far enough to hint at the curves hiding beneath. Her blond hair was yanked into a haphazard bun on the back of her head, long strands falling loose, like they were teasing me. Making my hands itch to yank out that rubber band and see just how much of her hair I could wrap around my fist. Grease was smudged on the curve of her cheekbone, and her mouth was plush and soft-looking, with the kind of lips a man dreamed of dragging his teeth across.

Her sun-kissed skin was golden from hours at the track, and those legs—fuck me—were long enough to make me want to sin. Even under the loose fabric, I could tell she had a body meant to be touched. Worshipped.

My cock was already hard enough to punch through my jeans, and I turned for a second to adjust myself, but I was so swollen, it didn't help much.

I didn't know her name. Didn't know her story. But I—

*Mine.*

Holy shit. The thought had come out of nowhere. Raw. Fierce. Possessive.

*Mine.*

My feet seemed glued to the ground, and I just stood there watching her, cataloging every detail like she was the last beautiful thing I'd ever see.

I wanted her on her knees. On her back. On top

of me. Wrapped around my fuckin' waist while I wrecked her body and carved my name into her soul.

Then she turned and caught me staring. Her blue eyes—fuck, they were unreal—locked onto mine. They widened for a half second before they narrowed and went cold.

She was not impressed. I bit back a grin.

Instead of blushing or looking away, she crossed her arms over her chest and tilted her head, leveling me with a look that said I wasn't shit.

I fucking loved it.

My cocky grin curved wide as I swaggered toward her. "Didn't know angels moonlighted as grease monkeys."

She gave me a slow once-over, unmoved. "Didn't know assholes came with fan clubs."

Barking a laugh, I stopped a few feet from her. "That how you talk to all the drivers? Or just the pretty ones?"

She arched a brow, tapping a wrench against her palm. "Only the ones dumb enough to nearly fishtail into the pit wall to show off."

"Wasn't showing off," I said, smirking. "Was proving a point."

"What point? That you have a death wish and no traction control?"

I stifled a laugh and leaned in slightly, lowering my voice. "You always this mouthy, or am I just special?"

Her cheeks flushed. A hint of pink across that sun-kissed skin. My grin deepened.

She lifted her chin, refusing to back down. "If you're going to drive like a maniac, at least try not to wreck anything important."

"Define important," I murmured, letting my gaze drop to her mouth.

She caught it, and her breath hitched. Not much. Just enough for a trained eye like mine to spot. She was affected. She just didn't want to be.

Cute.

Sexy.

Fucking dangerous.

Before I could push for more, I heard Kane's voice behind me. "Racer, you settling in okay?"

I turned to see him striding up, casual and unreadable. The girl beside me shifted instantly, her face softening as she lit up with a smile.

"Kane." She threw her arms around his neck, and he hugged her back tightly.

Something primal and ugly surged inside me.

*Mine.*

I didn't know what their connection was, but if

Kane didn't get his hands off her, I was going to break every bone in his body.

Then Kane pulled back and kissed the top of her head.

It took everything in me not to start by knocking out his teeth.

"You been keepin' the guys in line?" he asked in a teasing tone.

"Trying," she said with a smirk. "Some of them are idiots."

"Tell me something I don't know," he replied, then turned to me. "You met Emily yet?"

Emily. It was a beautiful name. And it fit her.

"No," I said, winking at her.

"One of my best mechanics."

Mechanic.

The conversation we'd had back at the Iron Rogues clubhouse came screaming back to me, and my stomach dropped. She was the mechanic he mentioned. The one who was his Road Captain's sister. A Redline King. Which meant that there could potentially be a big fucking obstacle between us.

"Em, meet Racer."

Emily turned to me again, her eyes narrowing. "This your new golden boy?"

Kane nodded. "One of the best."

She made a noncommittal noise. "We'll see."

Kane grinned and turned back to me. "She's better at fixing engines than most of my guys. Started wrenching when she was twelve."

I raised a brow. "That right?"

Emily's gaze didn't waver. "You break your ride, I'll fix it. You break your neck, that's on you."

I couldn't stop the smile that tugged at my lips. "What if I break your patience?"

"Then I'll break your face," she shot back.

I'd never wanted anyone more.

*Fuck.* I was in so much trouble.

**4**

---

EMILY

I should've walked away the second Kane finished introductions. But I didn't.

I must've been a glutton for punishment. Especially the kind that made heat curl low in my stomach.

I spent most of my time around guys as far back as I could remember, but I'd never reacted to one like this before. Then again, none of the guys I worked with looked like Racer.

After years of wondering if my libido was broken, I finally discovered what kind of guy got my engine revving at the absolute worst time. Tall and muscular with messy dark blond hair and green eyes that didn't miss much. And a body that came from adrenaline and grease, not vanity. The flames inked down his right arm made me wonder if he had more art beneath his slightly damp black tee.

"Emily," Kane said with a warning in his voice.

Racer waved him off. "It's fine."

Crossing my arms, I shifted my weight to one foot, unsure how to feel about him not minding my threats. "You sure he's not just here to collect phone numbers?"

Racer grinned, all cocky confidence and no shame. "Only if yours comes first."

Of course he had a quick comeback.

I kind of hated how easily he took our banter in stride. As though I wasn't being prickly on purpose. Like I didn't have a reason to be pissed that he needed to be here in the first place, let alone walking around the pit after fishtailing across the track and nearly kissing the damn barricade for attention.

Kane clapped him on the shoulder. "Careful, I wasn't kidding about her skills. Em knows the insides of these engines better than most drivers know their steering columns."

"Noted," Racer said, still looking at me like I was more interesting than the damn car next to us.

I refused to blush under his stare even though it

was hot enough to blame any color in my cheeks on the weather.

"As long as your golden boy knows how to keep four tires on the pavement, maybe he won't make my job harder," I muttered.

Racer chuckled behind me. "Wasn't aware I needed to impress you, angel."

"Never said you did," I shot back. "But you don't want to piss me off either."

Kane waited until Racer wandered off to check one of the Chevelles, then hooked two fingers around my elbow and tugged me a few steps away. Not far enough for anyone to notice, just so our voices wouldn't carry to the rest of our crew.

"He's gonna race, but that's not why I brought Racer down here," Kane said, low and serious.

I narrowed my eyes. "What do you mean?"

"He's bait."

My stomach flipped. "Bait?"

"We're trying to draw out whoever's behind the sabotage. Racer's flashy. Fast. The kind of driver that'll piss the right people off. Make 'em sloppy."

I blinked, stunned for a beat. "That's the plan? Toss the new guy onto the track and hope the bad guy bites?"

Kane's jaw flexed. "Trust me, it'll work. Racer can more than handle himself on and off the circuit. He's not just any guy behind the wheel. He's also an Iron Rogues enforcer."

Scrubbing my palms down my face, I heaved a deep sigh. "I still want to help. There are things I can do from the pit that a driver can't."

He shook his head, already stepping back. "Just let Racer handle it."

"Kane—" I started, but he was already walking away, shoulders tight and done with the conversation.

My fists clenched at my sides.

I hated being sidelined while some cocky out-of-town racer with fast hands and a flirty smile got handed the keys to the whole damn situation.

I was the one who'd been here from the beginning. Who knew these cars inside and out. Whose brother was lying in a hospital bed, barely hanging on.

I wanted to help find the people responsible for his crash more than anything, but Kane was my boss. And Mason's club president. He wasn't the kind of guy who'd be okay with me pushing my way into the situation, so I would just need to be sneaky about it behind the scenes. Sometimes you had to ask for forgiveness instead of permission, and I'd take the heat down the line if it came to that.

I stormed back toward one of the Chevelles, grabbing my tablet and tools like they were weapons instead of diagnostics gear.

Of course his road name was Racer. His club brothers might as well have called him Adrenaline McFlashy.

He was probably one of those golden boys who looked good behind the wheel, flashed a grin for the cameras, and didn't know jack about the machines he drove. Guys like that pushed too hard, burned through clutches, and blamed the crew when something snapped.

And now Kane had given him my brother's spot in our world.

I dropped to one knee beside the car, popping off the panel that gave me access to the rear suspension mount. I didn't even realize my hands were shaking until the ratchet slipped on the bolt and scraped across my knuckles.

"Careful." The low voice came from behind me.

Twisting around, I glared at him. "What do you want?"

Racer crouched next to me, hands on his knees as

he peered into the cavity I'd just exposed. "That bracket looks off. See the weld?"

I opened my mouth to snap something sarcastic, but I paused when I noticed how closely he was looking at the part in question. Turning back around, I flicked my gaze down, following his line of sight.

*Damn.* He was right.

One of the mounting brackets had the faintest hairline crack near the weld. Not visible at first glance, but enough that, under race stress, it could've snapped and launched the driver into a wall or another car.

"You have a good eye," I muttered, brushing my fingers over the fault line.

He didn't gloat. Just angled in a little closer. "Mind if I take a look at something?"

I huffed but scooted over slightly.

Racer leaned in and ran a fingertip along the bolt housing on the opposite side. Then he pulled a small flashlight from his back pocket and clicked it on.

"There." He pointed. "That scoring? Looks like someone used the wrong torque setting. Or maybe they just wanted it to look that way."

I blinked, then nudged him to the side so I could see better. Sure enough, there was a shallow ring on the metal, inconsistent with our tools.

My mouth went dry.

Someone had tampered with that bolt. Subtly enough that it could've passed inspections. But if the bracket failed mid-race...

*Crap.*

"You might've just saved someone's life," I said quietly.

Racer met my gaze for the first time in a way that felt real instead of flirtatious. "That's the idea."

I sat back on my heels, blowing out a breath. "Guess Kane brought in the right guy after all."

His mouth quirked into a half smile, but he didn't say anything.

And just like that, Racer wasn't the enemy anymore.

Kane headed back toward us, a grim set to his jaw that told me whatever conversation he'd just had hadn't gone how he wanted. His expression only grew stonier when I pointed out what we found on the Chevelle.

I straightened. "Kane, listen—"

"She should be in on this," Racer cut in before I could finish.

I blinked, surprised he beat me to it.

He didn't look away from Kane. "She knows these cars. She's sharp. And if someone's slipping past her, it means they're damn good. You want this asshole caught? You need her eyes on the rides."

Kane exhaled through his nose, clearly weighing his decision. Then he gave a curt nod. "Fine. But you help me keep an eye on Emily. Nothing better fucking happen to her. Understood?"

"It won't," Racer growled. "I won't let anyone hurt her."

Kane pointed at him. "You better not, or it'll be your ass. No matter what Fox will want as payback."

After growing up with an overprotective brother and another overprotective almost-brother, I knew better than to waste my breath saying I could take care of myself. Neither of them would listen.

When Kane walked off, I murmured, "Thanks for speaking up for me, Racer."

He turned toward me, something warm flickering in his green eyes. "Call me Jude."

I stared at him. "What?"

He gave me a half smile. "That's my name. Jude Iverson."

Most bikers I knew guarded their real names like state secrets, only letting family or people they'd known forever call them anything besides their road name. That he offered his so easily threw me even more than the pull I felt toward him. "Okay, Jude."

It tasted strange on my tongue, more personal than I expected. And way too distracting.

I turned back to the car before I did something stupid. Like say it again. Or worse—doodle Mrs. Emily Iverson on my tablet as though I was thirteen again.

## 5

RACER

The next evening, the Florida heat was a living thing—clinging to my skin while it wrapped me in a layer of grit, smoke, and engine oil. The track tonight was in the middle of nowhere, tucked behind a run-down warehouse and lined with barrel fires that flickered like the crowd's crackling energy. Asphalt crunched beneath my boots as I paced the length of the pit, waiting for my turn on the line.

This was my second race. Another qualifier. But this time, I wasn't just here to win—I was here to watch.

While Edge handled entry logistics, I used the prep hour to scope the scene. Some of the teams we were suspicious of were parked nearby. Haulers pulled open, crews bustling around engines, wiping sweat from their brows. Though they would appear casual to most, I could feel the tension surrounding them like a thick cloud.

Some had real strain on their faces, while others looked too calm, which put me on edge. People were usually either nervous because they had no fucking clue what was happening, or because they did.

I made my way through the pits slowly, stopping here and there to chat with a few of the team owners. Names Kane had flagged as ones we could maybe trust—guys who'd already lost drivers to suspicious wrecks. One of them, a grizzled man named Andy with a faded T-shirt that sported his team's logo and a voice like gravel, shook his head when I asked what he thought of the crashes.

"Doesn't make sense," he muttered, flicking the ash off his cigarette. "My boy, Fender, he's not the kind of driver to fuck up a corner like that. I watched that race three times. No fucking way did he lose control. Something else happened."

I nodded slowly. "You tell anyone else?"

He eyed me, chewing the inside of his cheek. "Not worth it. No proof to take to Kane. And if someone is fuckin' with this circuit, I don't want a target on my back."

"Too late," I said, clapping him on the shoulder.

"Eyes are already on all of us. Better to face the fucker head-on than wait to get picked off."

He looked at me like maybe I was suicidal but didn't argue. My gut impression was that we could trust Andy, but I'd confer with Kane about it after I had a full list.

By the time my turn rolled around, my body was restless, and I was ready to feel the engine under me again. The Chevelle was even crisper tonight than it had been at the last race. She'd been cleaned up, adjusted, and fine-tuned by one of Kane's top crew chiefs, and I could feel the responsiveness in every inch of her frame. She was fast, angry, and begging to be let loose. We made a perfect fucking team.

The starter gave the signal.

I slammed the accelerator and took off like I'd been shot out of hell.

This course was narrower than the last one, with more sharp corners and tighter pack racing, but I made a show of it. Let the others think they had a chance before I cut between them like a blade, my engine screaming, and tires kicking up clouds of rubber smoke as I drifted into the corners with just enough recklessness to make the crowd lose their shit. On the final lap, I downshifted and spun into the last turn sideways, just for the fuck of it, before hammering the gas and crossing the finish line two full seconds ahead of the next driver.

When I rolled back into the pit and climbed out with a crooked grin on my face, the roar of the crowd still echoed in my ears. But louder than that was the silence that followed me when I walked past some of the losers.

Two of them in particular looked like they'd seen a ghost. Pale, tight-jawed—fucking terrified. They whispered to their crew in low, frantic tones that set off alarm bells.

Edge appeared at my side out of nowhere.

"Those two were the favorites." He didn't even try to hide the satisfaction in his voice. "You just cost a shitload of people a lot of fucking money."

"Good," I said, keeping my senses alert to the people in my surroundings. "Let 'em know they've got something to lose."

Edge's eyes flicked to the side, narrowing. "What the fuck?"

I followed his gaze, and my gut twisted.

I'd noticed when Emily stepped out of the pit to grab something from the cart near the edge of the lot, away from the rest of the crew. But Edge had diverted my attention, and now she was boxed in by two big motherfuckers in dark hoodies. Wide shoulders, cold eyes, and radiating intimidation. They were the kind of guys who walked with the casual confidence of men used to getting their way. One leaned in close, speaking low and sharp to Emily.

She was stiff as steel, her chin lifted, refusing to show fear, but I saw the way her hand twitched at her side. A subtle tell that she was scared. *That's my girl.*

I was already moving, but when one of them grabbed her arm, I growled, "Fuck this," and sped up. Edge followed right behind me.

Once we reached her, I stepped between Emily and the taller of the two pricks—although I had at least two inches on him—and met his gaze dead-on.

I didn't even raise my voice. "You lost?" I asked, low and controlled. Deadly.

The guy sneered. "Just giving some advice to the girl here. She's been sticking her nose where it don't belong."

Keeping my expression unreadable, I tilted my head, letting the silence drag just long enough to tighten the noose, then murmured, "You have three seconds to walk away before I start snapping bones alphabetically, starting with your ankles and ending with your fucking spine."

He hesitated, but something in my tone must've gotten through.

Or maybe it was the fact that Edge stepped up beside me, hand resting near the blade sheathed at his belt, his expression almost bored. "When he's done, I'm gonna carve a smile across your throat and make you watch your own pulse bleed out in the dirt."

Whatever the reason, both thugs backed off and slunk away.

"Fucking cowards," I grunted. Bullies never stayed brave when someone stood taller.

Emily tried to thank me, but I waved her gratitude off—until I caught the tremor in her hands.

"Hey." I stepped in, reaching for her. "You okay?"

She jerked back slightly, cheeks pink, and her gaze darting over my shoulder for a second. "I'm fine. Don't—" Her voice cracked, and she whispered, "Don't let them see me like this. I don't want them thinking I'm weak."

Edge scoffed. "They're not stupid enough to believe that, Em."

Her expression said she didn't believe him. She inhaled slowly, but her hands were still trembling.

I slid my palm against hers and interlaced our fingers, already moving and grunted, "Come on."

She let me lead her away, keeping her head down, until we were around the corner behind a stack of shipping crates. No one could see us there—not crew, cameras, or asshole thugs looking for a reaction.

I pulled her against me, and she came without resistance. Nor did she fight me when I wrapped both arms around her and held her tight.

Her hands bunched in my shirt, and she buried her face in my chest, breathing shaky and quiet. I didn't say anything. Just held Emily and let her fall apart. She didn't make a sound, but I could feel the tears soaking my shirt.

A few minutes later, she finally exhaled and stepped back, wiping at her eyes. "Sorry," she muttered. Then she blew out a harsh breath and fisted her hands at her sides. "I just...ugh. I hate that I freaking cried. I hate that they scared me."

"They should've," I said, brushing her hair back from her cheek. "Those fuckers were threatening you. You don't have to be like stone every second of the day. Feeling something doesn't make you less."

She tried to scoff, but it wobbled. "You sound like my brother."

I leaned closer, my voice dropping to a whisper. "I sound better than your brother, angel. And a fuck of a lot more dangerous."

Her eyes widened just slightly, and I saw the flush spread down her throat. It was sexy as hell, and I wanted to follow the trail of color with my tongue. Instead, I muttered, "You don't have to blend in with the guys, baby. Fuck their opinions. You're not one of them."

Before I could stop myself, my fingers brushed her cheek and trailed to her collarbone, causing her to shiver. Her skin was as soft as silk, and her bright blue eyes had deepened to sapphire. Then my lips curled down at the thought of her standing out among the grease monkeys, and I blurted, "Never mind."

She blinked up at me. "Why?"

I hesitated, thinking about all the ways I could answer that. Ultimately, I settled on the truth. "Because I don't want other men looking at you like that. I don't want them wanting you. Fantasizing about my angel. Touching what's not theirs—even if it's only in their dreams."

Her lips parted, and her breath caught. "What... what do you mean?"

Lowering my head, I slid my hand to her waist.

"I don't share," I said, my voice a raspy whisper.

She didn't say a word. Just stared up at me, eyes wide, lips soft and parted, as though she was frozen on the edge of something dangerous and didn't know whether to jump or run.

Running wasn't a fucking option. Clarity slammed into me. I was never gonna let her go.

My eyes dropped to her lips, and I took hold of her chin, lifting her face so I could kiss her. Devour her. Fucking ruin her for anyone else and brand her mouth with mine. I was gonna give her a kiss she'd never forget.

"Racer." Edge's voice snapped around the corner, sharp and mocking. "Kane's headed this way. If you wanna keep your balls, maybe don't be caught making out with the girl he sees as a baby sister."

I rolled my eyes, but Emily tensed and immediately tried to pull away.

"Nope." I caught her wrist before she could flee and yanked her back against my chest.

She let out a tiny squeak, her eyes darting toward the open lane. "Kane'll see!"

I raised an eyebrow and reached around to hook my fingers into the back belt loop of her coveralls, holding her flush to me with a smirk.

"So?"

Before she could speak, Kane came around the corner, and I reluctantly let her step to the side, keeping a hold of her belt loop so she couldn't get away.

He stopped and looked us over with concern. "You two good?"

"Peachy," I said, voice smooth and relaxed.

He frowned and jerked a thumb over his shoulder. "Saw those two assholes leaving the pit a few minutes ago. You run into them?"

I bobbed my head once. "Been handled."

Edge didn't say a word, bless his twisted little heart.

Kane lifted his chin in acknowledgment. "Took me a minute, but I recognized them."

My brow lifted.

"They work for Dez Franklin."

"The small-time bookie that killed his way to the top and runs a crew now?" Edge asked with a deep scowl. "You think he's behind the betting syndicate?"

Kane nodded, but his attention had shifted to Emily. "You okay?"

"All good. But I should go. I have stuff to do back at the garage." She tried to take a step forward, but my fingers tightened around the loop, foiling her escape attempt. I just smiled when she tossed me a cute, disgruntled frown.

"I'll give you a ride," Kane offered, already pulling out his keys.

I cut in, not giving her a chance to answer. "She's riding with me."

Kane paused. Then blinked before slowly looking at me, as though he wasn't sure he'd heard that right.

"You're letting her on your bike?" he asked, clearly surprised.

"She's like your family," I replied easily, though in my head, I was muttering about how she was not his fucking family...she was mine.

Kane hesitated, then nodded, accepting the logic. "Appreciate it. Gives me time to talk to some of the other owners."

He walked off, tossing a wave over his shoulder.

Edge waited until he was gone before whistling low. "You are so fucked, brother."

"Fuck off," I muttered, but my hand didn't move from Emily's hip.

Edge's grin widened. "I mean, fuck, next thing we know she'll be driving your bike and wearin' your balls on a chain."

"You done?" I glared at him.

He kept laughing.

Ignoring him, I took Emily's hand and tugged her toward the lot. My hog was waiting, the seat shining under the low floodlights.

She was silent, her gaze locked on my bike.

I smiled. "Pass your muster?"

She nodded slowly as she continued to inspect the Harley, a smile playing at her lips. "I'm a little jealous."

I laughed. "You should see my '79 Triumph Bonneville back in Old Bridge. Restored her myself."

Emily lit up and smiled. "I love vintage motorcycles. There's just something especially sexy about them."

Slipping my arm around her waist, I pulled her up against my body. "Yeah, but they can't compare to you."

"Me?" She looked up at me with a shocked expression that made me wonder just how often she'd been told how beautiful and womanly she was. I kind of wanted to beat the shit out of her brother, and even Kane and Edge, for treating her "like one of the guys." Even if she'd acted as if that was what she wanted.

I let her go—grudgingly—and grabbed the extra

helmet, holding it out. "You're sexy as fuck, angel. Now, get on. I'll take you back to the garage."

Her cheeks flushed adorably. And even though she didn't say a word, her eyes held mine just a moment longer than necessary.

And that was enough to confirm that I wasn't the only one feeling this chemistry.

Whatever this was, it was complicated and about to get messy.

And I didn't give a single fuck.

**6**

---

EMILY

The Harley's engine vibrated through me as I held on to Jude. Riding on the back of his hog wasn't anything like I expected. Completely different from being on my brother's motorcycle, which was the only thing I could compare this to.

Most bikers didn't let just anyone ride with them, at least that was how it was in the Redline Kings. Putting a woman who wasn't related to you on the back of your bike meant something to my brother's club. I didn't know if it meant the same to Jude, though.

By the time we pulled into the side bay at Kane's garage, my nerves were tangled up with something sharp and aching that had nothing to do with fear.

My pulse was unsteady, and I was keyed up from how aware I was of the man.

I swung off and stepped back quickly, trying to steady myself before I said something stupid.

"I need to check my brother's Mustang," I blurted. "The Shelby GT350R-C. I've been over it a dozen times, but...maybe you'll see something I missed. If you have time to look?"

Jude gave a short nod and followed me inside.

The Mustang sat under a canvas tarp, untouched since I'd gone over it. I hesitated before peeling the material back, part of me still hoping we'd find something less nefarious to explain Mason's crash.

"What've you already checked?" he asked, voice quiet but steady.

I rattled off the list automatically. "Brake lines, suspension, throttle linkage, fuel system. The works."

When I finally looked up, Jude watched me with something that looked a lot like admiration. "Let's take a deeper look. Pop the hood."

We were quiet as we got to work, but the silence between us wasn't awkward. We were focused. Intent.

The longer we worked, the harder it was to ignore him. Which was weird for me because I'd never had trouble focusing when I was in a garage. Give me a busted engine, and the rest of the world disappeared. But tonight, with Jude beside me, every turn of his wrench tugged at my attention like a magnet. I felt the heat coming off his body each time he leaned past me. I was hyper-aware of the stretch of his muscles, the flames tattoo rippling on his forearm. And the scent of him—a heady mixture of oil, sweat, and something dark and woodsy that lingered.

It was distracting. Maddening. And entirely new.

I'd just started checking the fuel rail and injector housing—nothing cracked, nothing loose—when Jude's voice broke through my thoughts.

"Emily," he said, low but firm.

I glanced over and found him crouched low on the passenger side. He was frowning at a cluster of exposed wires he'd pulled free from the fuse panel, the beam of his small flashlight making the colors gleam.

"This is wrong," he muttered.

"What do you mean?"

He gestured for me to come closer. I moved toward him fast, wiping my hands on my thighs as I knelt beside him.

"See this junction?" He pointed with the butt of the flashlight. "This splice. Factory harness doesn't route this way. Someone reran part of the feedback loop."

I leaned in, heart thudding. "Are you sure?"

"Positive." His jaw ticked. "This isn't just rerouted—it's bridged. Fail-safe input's been bypassed so it'd register clean even if the engine started to fail. None of the warnings would've triggered. If Axle's engine started to cook or misfire, the ECU wouldn't throw a code. The telemetry would've looked normal right up until it didn't."

I stared at the spliced wires, blinking hard. "They rigged the feedback so the car lied to him."

"Exactly," he agreed in a grim tone. "Confuse it so the driver doesn't get a warning until it's too late.

"And look there."

I wiped grime off the side panel and looked closer. There was a melted toggle behind the cage bar. "Holy crap. With the fuel shutoff bypassed— that's why the engine kept pulling until it snapped."

Jude's green eyes had darkened to nearly black, rage clearly boiling inside him. "And if they messed with anything else..."

As he trailed off, I was even more determined to

find every single thing wrong with my brother's car. "Let's keep looking."

He nodded. "As long as it takes."

After a couple more hours of both of us going over the Shelby with a fine-tooth comb, I remembered the injector housing I'd been checking out. I reached in and tugged the injector loom farther out, my eyes narrowing. "This isn't right."

Jude rounded the hood of the mangled Mustang to peer over my shoulder. "Holy shit. Whoever did this dialed back the injector cycle. Just enough to lean the mix under load."

My mind raced. "Too much air, not enough fuel..."

"Engine runs hot," he muttered. "Real hot. You're cooking pistons before you even know something's wrong. At top speed, that kind of strain—"

"He'd lose power coming into the turn," I finished, breath shallow. "No warning light. No dash alert. Just a stall or a knock right when he needed control."

Jude sat back on his heels and stared at the wreckage like he could see Mason in the seat. "They built a fucking trap," he said flatly. "Did just enough to make it look like Axle screwed up. No code, no fail-safe, no brake warning. Everything set to fry the car at the worst possible second."

"And now the data's gone," I added, my mouth going dry. "No digital proof. They got exactly what they wanted."

"Except for one thing." Jude looked up at me, his expression unreadable but intense. "This wasn't just about making your brother lose. They wanted to make sure he didn't walk away."

My stomach dropped, the truth settling in my chest, sharp and cold. We found what I'd suspected all along. But hearing it out loud made the ground shift beneath me.

"They wanted him dead," I whispered.

The words hung in the air between us, too heavy to take back. Too real to ignore.

I braced my hands against the frame of the car, trying to steady myself. "I knew it wasn't an accident. But everyone kept telling me to let it go. That Mason must've made a mistake. Except for Kane. And you."

"You were right all along."

Something in me cracked at the quiet, hard certainty in his tone. But my reaction didn't make me any less resolved. Only more so.

Someone had tried to kill my brother, and we were going to find out who. Together.

The weight of it all should've felt crushing, but I somehow felt...hopeful. And exhausted.

I'd barely slept since Mason's crash. We'd been working on his car for hours, plus the time we'd spent at the race earlier tonight. My body ached, and sweat clung to the back of my neck. I leaned against the edge of the Mustang, too wired to sit and too raw to pretend we hadn't just uncovered proof that someone tried to murder my brother.

"Fuck, it's hot as hell in here, even in the middle of the damn night." Jude reached behind his neck and tugged his shirt over his head.

I looked away, but not for long. Even with what we'd just discovered, his pull was too strong.

The overhead light caught the sweat beading on his chest, the ridges of muscle across his stomach, and the checkered flags inked on his right pec.

He reached for a rag, wiping his hands, then glanced up. And caught me staring.

A smirk curved the corner of his mouth as he slowly stalked closer, his gaze fixed on mine as though he could see straight through me.

His voice was low and rough as he murmured, "You keep looking at me like that, angel, and I'm gonna bend you over this car and show you exactly what happens when you tempt a man who doesn't play fair."

My breath caught at the sensual threat.

I didn't move. Didn't look away. And I definitely didn't deny that I was looking at Jude as though I wanted to eat him up.

I should've said something—anything—to defuse the heat rising between us, but my tongue was dry and my brain had short-circuited somewhere between the tattoo I hadn't already seen and the way he called me angel.

My gaze dropped to his mouth, and it took me a moment to realize how big of a mistake that was. Now, all I could do was think about what his lips would feel like pressed against mine, his tongue sliding into my mouth. The heat of his bare skin. The weight of him. The rasp of his voice in my ear as he made good on that threat.

"Last chance to back away, angel," he murmured, his tone softer now. Almost teasing.

I was so tempted to give in and take the distraction he was offering me, but a little voice in my head reminded me about what we'd just discovered. I couldn't help but wonder if kissing him while my brother was fighting for his life would make me a horrible person. Or if what happened to Mason was the reason I should go for it. Because I'd been given a rough reminder that life was too short.

Swallowing hard, I pushed off the car and tried to force oxygen back into my lungs.

The air between us crackled, too charged for comfort. One wrong move, and we'd go up in flames.

# 7

RACER

Her blue eyes were dazed, and her lips parted just enough to tempt me into madness. I stared at her pulse kicking at her throat, fast and fluttering like she was seconds from bolting. Or begging.

I was barely holding on by a thread, so I didn't give her the chance to decide.

I yanked her to me by the front of her coveralls, crushed my mouth to hers, and let everything I'd been holding back flood out of me like a fucking tidal wave. I swallowed her gasp as her hands went instinctively to my chest as though she was going to push me away.

But she didn't.

Instead, her fingers stroked up and down my chest.

*Fuck.* I was about to lose every shred of control I'd been clinging to.

Nothing about the way I kissed her was soft. Nothing hesitant. It was filthy, hungry, and desperate. My breath was heavy and labored, the flavor of her clinging to my tongue like I'd tasted something forbidden and couldn't stop going back for more.

Her lips were plush and warm, yielding under mine, and when I slid my tongue across the seam of her mouth, she opened for me on a breathy sound that had my cock pressing against my zipper.

My hand slid up her spine, dragging her closer. Her chest heaved, and her knees buckled just enough that I had to angle her back, pinning her against the Mustang's fender. I braced one hand against the car beside her head, the other wrapped firmly around her hip, and my fingers curled possessively into the thick cotton fabric.

Fuck me, she was perfect. Mouthy, smart, and bold. But right now, she clung to me, arching her back and pressing her soft curves against me.

I slipped a hand between us and slowly lowered the zipper on her coveralls, overwhelmed with the need to feel her hot, silky skin. When it was halfway down, I leaned back to look down at her. My gaze followed the smooth line of her throat, down to the teasing swell of cleavage that made my brain short out.

She watched me through hooded blue eyes and licked her lips, making me groan. My fingers gripped her hip harder.

"What did I say about looking at me like that, angel?" I growled, voice rough and low, "Keep tempting me, and I'm gonna bend you over this car and make you forget every fucking name but mine."

Her thighs squeezed together, and her breath caught. She whimpered my name as though it was torn from her lungs. Her fingers dug into my shoulders, and she let out a tiny, gasping moan that sounded like sin itself. Her hips involuntarily rocked into mine, her body practically begging to be filled.

I crushed our mouths together again, devouring her as if she were my first meal after years of starvation.

She gave me another needy moan, then shocked the hell out of me when she bit my bottom lip, sending lightning through my spine. I rocked my hips into her instinctively, making her gasp. That sass-meets-shyness edge of hers was doing dangerous things to my control.

"You're killing me, angel," I rasped against her lips, my voice gritty with restraint.

Her breath caught. "Then die quieter."

I barked a laugh and fell even harder for her.

Sealing my mouth over hers once more, I kissed her slower—and dirtier. I explored her mouth as though it belonged to me, like I had every right to learn the shape of it, every moan she made, every tremble of her lips. My free hand slid down her hip, fingers flexing as I gripped her ass.

Then my mouth dipped, trailing down her neck, my stubble scraping against soft skin as she arched into me. I muttered her name against her collarbone, tasting the salt of her skin before I moved lower. My lips glided along the curve of one breast, then I dragged my tongue along the edge of her bra until she let out another one of those shaky little breaths that sounded like surrender.

She shifted restlessly against me, and the scent of her—engine grease and something warm and womanly underneath—hit me hard.

I needed her under me.

On top of me.

Bent over this car, her thighs trembling as I wrecked her from behind.

I was seconds from losing it. About to give in to every filthy thought I'd had since the second I laid eyes on her. I was gonna claim her so hard there would be no doubt she was mine.

"Jude," she breathed, voice wrecked.

"You taste like sin," I growled, burying my face in that sweet valley between her tits and forgetting who the fuck I was for a minute.

Then a voice shattered it all like a brick through glass.

"For fuck's sake. Again?"

I froze.

Emily squeaked.

And I damn near snapped someone's neck.

I whirled around and shoved her behind me, so I was shielding her from anyone else's eyes. My other hand was already twitching toward the blade tucked behind my waistband.

Edge stood a few yards away, smug and amused, arms crossed over his chest like this was the best show he'd seen all year. His wicked grin was full of teeth. He was way too pleased with himself for a man who clearly didn't value his life.

He raised his brows, taking in the scene—my flushed face, Emily's tousled hair and wild eyes, the way I was clearly blocking her from view like a damn linebacker.

"Really?" he said, voice dry as fuck. "I turn a

corner, and it's like walking into a fucking porn shoot. That poor car is never gonna run right again."

"You trying to get your spine bent backward, asshole?" I snarled, eyes narrowing.

"You ever think about locking the door?" he quipped back, arching a brow. "Or were you planning to charge admission?"

I glared at him, murder in my veins. "Do you want to die, Edge?"

He just grinned. "I mean, not tonight. But if you're offering to beat me to death with a torque wrench, I'd rather it not be because I interrupted you trying to test-fire your rocket in her ignition system."

"Keep running your mouth, and it's gonna be a tire iron up your ass," I snapped.

Edge waved me off, unbothered. "Relax, lover boy. I only came by to grab you cause Kane wants a word."

"Of course he fucking does," I muttered.

"Said it's urgent." Edge rocked back on his heels, still grinning. "You know, in case you need a reason to stop feeling her up like you forgot what self-control is. Just long enough to be useful."

Emily let out a strangled sound behind me, half laughter, half mortification, and buried her face in my back.

I glared at Edge as though I was mentally fitting him for a shallow grave.

"You're walking a real thin fucking line," I warned in a low, lethal voice.

He snorted and wandered off, still laughing to himself.

I turned back to Emily, who hid behind me, cheeks flaming red. Her hands were fisted at her sides, breathing uneven, like she was trying to decide whether to run.

"I'll let Kane know I'm following you home first," I said. It wasn't a question.

Her head snapped up. "What?"

"You heard me." I put my shirt back on, reached for her hand, and started leading her toward the front of the garage. "You're not walking or driving alone tonight, not after earlier."

"But Jude—"

"No arguments."

She huffed, muttering something that might've been "bossy jerk," but she'd clearly figured out I wasn't budging because she let me lead her to the parking lot anyway.

Her car was already there, tucked neatly in one of the back rows. I waited while she got in, then climbed on my bike and trailed her the whole way.

Her house wasn't far, only a few minutes from the Redline Kings compound. But it was just long enough for the wind to cool the fire still simmering under my skin. And for me to remember that I didn't want to scare Emily by pushing too fast, even if my whole body still hummed from the feel of her under my hands.

She parked her car in the narrow gravel strip beside the house she mentioned she shared with her brother, and I pulled my bike up next to her. The porch light was on, the small front yard quiet. A single potted plant hung by the door, swaying gently in the breeze.

Emily climbed out of her car, brushing her hands on her hips like she didn't know what to do with them. Her coveralls were still rumpled, her cheeks pink, and her lips swollen from my kiss.

I stepped off my bike and closed the distance between us in three strides—backing her up against the side of her car and cupping her face in my hands.

"You okay?" I asked, voice softer now.

She nodded and looked up at me from under her thick lashes. "I...yeah. Good night."

I raised a brow and growled, "Not done yet, angel."

She blinked. "What?"

Instead of answering, I crushed my mouth over hers.

She kissed me back with a low, breathless moan, melting into me as though she'd been waiting all day for this. The sound made my knees lock and my cock throb in my jeans. I kissed her until she was breathless, her eyes half lidded, lips kissed raw.

My mouth was rough and bruising. Possessive. My hands splayed along her hips, fingers flexing, anchoring her to me because I felt like I'd lose my fucking mind if I had to let her go. Her arms came around my shoulders, pulling me closer, until I could feel her every breath, every tremble, every pulse of heat that radiated from her. She was like a fucking drug.

I kissed her until she couldn't stand up straight. Until her lips were swollen, her knees were weak, and she was clinging to me as though she didn't ever want me to stop.

When I finally pulled back, her eyes were glazed, her lips wet, and her chest heaving.

I brushed my thumb across her cheek. "Lock the door behind you."

She nodded, dazed. "Okay."

I didn't trust myself to say anything else. Just turned and walked away, every step heavier than it should've been. When I reached my bike, I waited for her to go inside before swinging a leg over the seat. Then I peeled off into the dark—her taste still on my lips, her scent still in my lungs, and my cock still as hard as steel in my jeans.

This girl was gonna ruin me.

Yeah.

I was in so much fucking trouble.

## 8

RACER

I stood on the upper platform of the crew box with Kane, Edge, and Emily, my arms braced against the metal railing as we watched one of Kane's boys tear through the course in the final race before mine. Miller was a Redline King, a hell of a driver, and one of Kane's oldest friends. I'd met him years back when I started racing pro. He had a quick wit and was smoother behind the wheel than most people were on their best day walking. We'd become good friends.

"Fucking hell. The air here is thick enough to chew," I griped.

My clothes had become a second skin, and the humidity made every breath feel like it had weight. It was nearly ten p.m., but the floodlights overhead lit the entire lot as though it were high noon in hell.

I used the bottom of my shirt to wipe away the sweat trickling down the sides of my face. When I looked up, I caught Emily eyeing my abs and grinned. Her gaze bounced up to mine when I dropped the damp fabric, and I winked, letting her know she'd been caught ogling. Not that I minded.

Her cheeks bloomed red, but she just shrugged and turned back to watching the race.

*Damn.* Everything about this woman tempted me.

Shaking my head, I chuckled and returned my attention to the cars.

Miller was in the lead, as expected. His silver and red Dodge Challenger glinted under the lights, dipping and diving through turns with calculated aggression. But as he came into the third hairpin, something was off.

I felt it in my gut before I could name it. Call it instinct born of years of racing. Years of wrecks. And years of watching men die for less than a split-second mistake.

Miller should've braked, throttled back, and clipped the inside curve. Instead, the car surged.

"Did he just...?" Emily's voice was tight.

Dread sat in my stomach like a lead weight.

The engine growled, louder than it should've. The car didn't downshift. It lurched and overcorrected. He swerved to avoid clipping the wall, and I saw the moment he tried to stop—desperately stabbing the brakes, steering into the skid—but the Charger didn't respond.

"The lights on the dash are still lit up," I told Kane, already moving.

"What the fuck—" Kane bit out as he followed.

The car twisted again, then slammed nose-first into the barrier on the far end of the track, just shy of the pit entrance. The crowd roared in confusion and panic as the impact sent the car spinning out, tires locked, body rattling.

Then the worst happened.

The front end caught fire. Not just smoke. Flames.

"FUCK!" I started running.

Kane was at my heels, shouting into his comm. Edge jumped off the platform, cutting through the pit crew like a knife.

Miller's car had stalled partially sideways. Fire danced from beneath the hood, licking toward the windshield, bright orange against the gloss of steel. I slid across the asphalt, my boots skidding as I reached the driver's side.

The fucking engine was still running. That wasn't supposed to happen. I yanked on the door, but it was locked—jammed from the impact. Smoke was filling the cabin fast.

"Miller!" I shouted, pounding on the glass. His eyes were fluttering—barely conscious.

"Shut it down!" Kane roared behind me.

"I fucking *can't!*" Edge shouted back, trying the kill switch near the wheel well.

Emily was suddenly beside us, fire extinguisher in hand, blasting the flames near the hood as I shouted at Miller again, pounding harder on the window. My blood was surging with white-hot adrenaline.

"Stand back!" I bellowed, hauling back with everything I had and slamming my boot into the side window once, twice—glass spiderwebbed—then a third time until it shattered inward. Miller would have some cuts, but they'd be nothing compared to the burns if we didn't get him the fuck out of that car.

Flames popped somewhere beneath the engine block, and a fresh tongue of fire shot toward the windshield.

*Shit! Shit! Shit!*

Edge reached through the busted window and popped the latch from the inside, then I yanked the door open. Kane grabbed Miller's arm as I used the knife from my waistband to cut the harness.

Miller was limp. Singed and bleeding. But still alive.

We dragged him out seconds before the flames reached the fuel line. I felt the heat change—the pressure shift—and I shoved Kane hard just as the entire front end detonated.

The blast threw me back, blinding my eyes with the sudden light. I landed hard on my shoulder, ears ringing, and the world reeling.

And that was when the rage hit.

Not just from the pain in my ribs or the raw scorch of my palms from dragging Miller out of a burning coffin—but the truth I was now certain of.

This wasn't a performance failure. And it wasn't some random malfunction.

Someone had fucked with that car. And they had meant to kill him.

Not sideline him. Not make a statement. Fucking *kill*. Just like they'd tried with Emily's brother.

I pushed myself to my feet, blood thudding behind my ears, and my hands were shaking.

Whether it was from the impact or fury didn't really matter.

Kane called for medics as he knelt over Miller, his expression twisted into something half feral. Edge paced, fists clenching and unclenching, his face dark with murderous intent. Emily held the extinguisher with white knuckles, her mouth pressed tight, eyes locked on Miller.

Sirens sliced through the roar of the crowd—the firemen on their way to join the others currently trying to douse the fire.

"You see it?" I asked, voice low and ragged, looking at Kane. "That delay? He tried to kill the engine, and it didn't respond."

Kane's eyes snapped to mine. "Son of a bitch. An ECU override."

I scrubbed my hands over my face. "Had to be. And a fuel line rupture. Maybe the seal. It was fucking deliberate."

"That was a hit."

I nodded slowly, my eyes returning to my friend who was being loaded into an ambulance on a stretcher. "They wanted him dead, Kane. Not out of the race. Fucking dead."

Edge stalked over to join us, his eyes black with

rage. "The explosion was too clean. Someone planned this."

"They're making a point," I growled, watching the last of the car collapse inward. "And I fucking got it."

This wasn't just sabotage. This was a message.

It was for all of us, but especially for *me*.

That was a bullet meant to graze the side of my skull.

*We see you. Back off. Or you're next.*

I stared at the flames as the medics slammed the doors shut on the rig, the wail of the ambulance already blaring in the background. The sound of the impact was still in my ears, the scraping metal like nails on a chalkboard. And the sight of the car when the engine refused to shut down even as fire ate through the hood played on a loop in my mind.

It was the kind of thing you never forgot because it was tattooed into your fucking soul.

For a few minutes, I didn't speak. Didn't blink. Just watched.

Until I felt Emily beside me, her fingers brushing my arm.

I turned slowly toward her. The wrath inside me didn't ebb, but just seeing her next to me, unharmed, brought relief.

There was soot on her cheekbone, and her hair had fallen out of its bun, hanging loose around her face. Her spine was rigid, her jaw was clenched tight, and her cheeks flushed from heat. She looked pissed, determined, and so fucking brave. But I could see the fear swimming in her eyes, something she allowed only me to see.

Needing to touch her, I brushed my thumb over her cheek, clearing away some of the ash. I wanted to comfort her and offer reassurance, but all I could think about was blood.

"My friend almost died tonight," I said, my ragged voice quiet and even. "That was one of us in that car. One of our own. Again."

She nodded, her lip trembling slightly, but she still didn't break. Not even when she whispered, "It was just like that."

"What was, angel?"

"My brother's accident. It was so similar..."

*Shit.* It hadn't occurred to me that this would bring that memory screaming back. I had no fucking idea how she held it together, and it showed me just how damn strong she was.

"They were trying to scare us," I growled, teeth bared. "They fucked up because I don't get scared, I get angry. And I get fucking justice."

Edge stepped up next to me, his jaw flexing. "Went after another Redline King. Doesn't get more personal."

"Yeah," I said, my voice sharper than steel. "And now I'm gonna make it fucking messy."

I didn't bother trying to rein in my rage and deadly intent. The warnings had been delivered, but they were like a red flag being waved in front of an angry bull.

If Dez Franklin's crew was behind this, they'd made one very critical mistake.

They'd tried to kill another brother.

Now they were *mine*.

And I wasn't walking away until every last one of them bled.

## 9

### EMILY

In the wake of Miller's accident, Jude's playful smirk was gone. So was the cocky edge and sarcastic charm. What was left was something sharp and dangerous. Lethal.

But also steady. That was the part that got to me the most.

Kane and Edge were quick, but Jude had got to Miller first.

I was still trembling, trying to breathe through the memory of smoke, fire, and the awful sound of crunching metal that threw me back to Mason's crash.

I kept my gaze on Jude, and it grounded me. Anchored me in a way nothing else could.

He was pissed. I could feel it rolling off him in

waves, but his control never slipped. And when his hand brushed mine—just briefly, enough to check if I was okay—I nearly broke.

Jude somehow seemed to know exactly what I needed.

Wrapping his hand around my wrist, he murmured, "Gonna take Emily to the clubhouse."

"Good call." Kane shot me a concerned look. "Safest place for her to be right now."

I was still replaying everything when we started walking toward the lot.

We were only halfway to his bike when it happened.

A flash of headlights. The roar of an engine. And a blacked-out vehicle flying toward us way too fast for this area.

"Emily!" Jude yanked me back hard.

I stumbled against him, my heart leaping into my throat. The car sped past, close enough that the breeze it left behind whipped my hair around my face.

"What the hell?" I breathed, looking up at him.

His expression was carved from stone.

"I don't know if that was meant for you or me," he muttered, his voice low and deadly. "But they're gonna pay for getting that close to you."

He didn't wait for my response—just grabbed my hand and led me toward his bike. And when I climbed on behind him, I somehow felt safe.

The ride to the Redline Kings compound was short. I'd been here more times than I could count, but riding through the gate on the back of Jude's bike felt different.

Jude killed the engine, climbed off, and reached for me before I could dismount on my own.

"You're staying here tonight," he commanded, voice low and firm.

"I'm fine—"

"I don't care. You're not leaving until I know it's safe."

I blinked at the finality in his tone. Even if I had the energy to push back, there wasn't room for argument. "Okay."

His phone rang as we walked toward the clubhouse. Pulling it out of the inner pocket of his cut, he glanced at the screen. "It's Kane."

I couldn't hear the other side of the conversation, but my brows arched when Jude replied, "I'll find you after she's settled and not a minute before."

Nobody talked to Kane like that, but Jude didn't seem to care. Tapping the screen to end the call, he shoved his cell back in his pocket.

"I probably know the place better than you," I pointed out. "So you don't need to help get me settled."

"Still gonna do it," he insisted.

Nobody was around when Jude led me inside and down a wide hallway I'd never had a reason to explore before. We stopped at a door near the back.

"My room," he muttered, unlocking it. "You're safe here."

I would've been fine in my brother's room too. But I didn't suggest that. Not when a big part of me wanted to stay exactly where Jude put me.

Jude shut the door behind us and leaned his weight against it for a second, his eyes scanning the room before finally landing on me. "Sit tight. Rest. I'll be back soon."

My brows lifted. "Where are you going?"

"To deal with Kane." He straightened. "Don't open that door for anyone but me."

I shook my head with a soft laugh. "This is my brother's club. The president is practically another brother to me. No Redline King would ever hurt me."

"Good," he muttered. Then he was gone.

Rolling my eyes at his overprotectiveness, I decided to use my alone time wisely. The room Kane had given Jude—with its en suite bathroom—was a sign of how much he respected him.

I took a quick shower to wash off the scent of smoke that clung to my skin. Wrapping a towel around me, I realized the downside of not driving myself to the compound. I didn't have anything else to wear except my coveralls, which were filthy with grease, soot, and fire suppressant.

Spotting a black duffel in the closet, I dug through Jude's things for a tee and pair of sweats. I had just tugged them on when the door opened again.

I whirled around and let out a breath I didn't realize I was holding.

My gaze scanned his muscular body.

Quirking a brow, he asked, "What're you lookin' for?"

"Any signs that you and Kane got into a fight."

Jude smirked. "Kane won't interfere. Not as long as I keep my promise."

I narrowed my eyes. "What promise?"

"Club business."

"Seriously?" I huffed. "I hate when my brother pulls that crap, so don't expect me to just accept that two-word explanation and not ask any more questions."

"Give me a promise of your own, and maybe I'll tell you more."

"What kind of promise?" I asked suspiciously.

"After what happened back at the track, you're not leaving this clubhouse alone," he explained. "If I'm not with you, I want you to wear my spare cut."

I gasped, stunned by what he was asking. "Why?"

"It'll give you another layer of protection." He stalked over to me and gripped my hips. "And I protect what's mine."

He didn't give me a chance to overthink this. The moment I swayed toward him, Jude's mouth claimed mine. Hard and deep with no hesitation.

There was no well-meaning interruption this time. Only the two of us in a room that had a big bed that he quickly backed me toward without breaking the kiss. His hands ran down my sides before gripping my thighs and lifting me as though I weighed nothing. I hit the mattress with a gasp, and he followed, covering me completely.

My thighs instinctively widened to cradle his hips, and there was no missing how much he wanted me with his hard length pressed against my core.

I let out a little whimper of protest when he ended the kiss, and he pressed his forehead against mine. Fierce desire shone from his green eyes, making them a shade darker. "You feel almost too fucking good beneath me, angel."

A surge of feminine satisfaction rushed through me as I twined my arms around his neck. "Is that even possible?"

"Starting to think just about anything is when it comes to you." He brushed his lips against mine. "Never felt this kinda pull before."

Neither had I, but I had a feeling he didn't mean it the same way. At a full dozen years older than me —and being as ridiculously sexy as he was—the odds of Jude being a virgin too were probably the same as winning a billion dollars in the lottery without buying a ticket—zero.

"Maybe we should do something about it," I suggested.

He stroked his thumb across my bottom lip. "Don't go shy on me now. Tell me what you want, baby."

"You," I whispered, rocking my hips against him. "I want to see how hot the passion between us can burn."

"Prepare to be scorched," he growled.

That was all the warning I got before he tunneled his hand under the shirt I borrowed to drag it over my head and toss it onto the floor. I hadn't put my bra back on, so my breasts were bared to him. The tips pebbled beneath his hungry gaze, tightening even more when he dipped his head to suck one deep into his mouth.

"Whoa." My back arched off the mattress at the shock of pleasure that went straight to my core.

Letting go of my nipple with a pop, he smirked up at me. "Like that?"

"Uh-huh," I breathed, clutching his shoulders.

I felt his lips curve when he shifted to the other side, nibbling and swirling his tongue around my nipple while I moaned beneath him.

"Fucking love how responsive you are for me, angel," he mumbled against my skin as he kissed his way down my stomach, leaving a trail of goose bumps in his wake.

He licked along the waist of the pair of sweatpants I'd snagged from his bag, and my inner walls clenched with each swipe of his tongue. When he tugged the soft material, I lifted my hips so he could pull the pants off my legs. Leaving them wrapped around my ankles, he wedged himself between my legs and buried his face in my pussy.

"Damn," he groaned. "You taste fucking fantastic."

I threaded my fingers through his dark blond hair. "That feels amazing."

"Good, 'cause I'm gonna want to eat this sweet pussy every chance I get."

He slid his tongue through my wetness, and when he circled my clit, I gasped, "Jude."

"That's right, angel. Let me know how much you like havin' my mouth on your pussy," he urged before devouring me again.

He licked and sucked, stiffened his tongue to plunge it in my core, and swirled it around my clit. Over and over again until I was writhing beneath him in need. When he finally pinched my sensitive bundle of nerves, I flew over the edge, screaming his name, "Yes, oh yes, Jude!"

My entire body stiffened, my thighs locking around his head as he ate me through my orgasm. The first one any man had ever given me.

The thought echoed in my head as he yanked the sweats off my ankles and quickly stripped out of his clothes. He was kneeling between my legs, his fist wrapped around his dick when I blurted, "I'm a virgin."

Possessiveness flared in his eyes. "Am I the only man who's tasted your pussy, too?"

"Yes."

My confession didn't scare him away—it did the opposite instead.

"Didn't think it was possible to want you more than I already did, angel. But then you went and told me nobody else has ever felt you wrapped around their cock." He notched the tip of his dick at my entrance. "I'm the only one who gets to hear your screams of pleasure. See you fall apart for them."

"Uh-huh," I gasped as he inched forward, my nails digging into his shoulders.

"Because you're mine."

He punctuated his claim with a quick thrust of his hips, ripping through my innocence with one powerful surge. The pain wasn't as bad as I expected, probably because it came on the heels of a mind-blowing orgasm and he didn't give me the chance to tense up.

"Sorry, angel."

I gave him a jerky nod and took a few deep breaths before I murmured, "I'm okay."

"You sure?"

I wriggled my hips a little, relieved that only the slightest twinge of pain was quickly overpowered by pleasure. "Yeah."

That was all the encouragement he needed to

slowly drag his dick out of my wet heat before inching back in again. "Still good?"

"Good doesn't begin to describe it."

"Thank fuck," he grunted. "I'm fucking dying here, baby."

"Then don't hold back," I urged. "Gimme all you've got."

He picked up the pace, and I flung my head back against the pillow as he powered in and out of me. It wasn't long before my cries echoed around us.

"That's right, angel. Let me hear you. Wanna know you're enjoyin' this as much as I am."

"Jude, yes! Oh yes! Please, I'm so close."

He slid his hand between us to pinch my clit, and waves of intense pleasure crashed over me. My pussy clamped hard around his dick, and he anchored himself deep as he went over the edge with me. "Fuck yeah, baby. That's right. Milk the come from my cock just like that."

He stayed inside me until we both caught our breaths. Then he pulled out and shifted on the mattress to pull me into his arms. Between the adrenaline rush from the crash at the race and two intense orgasms, my lids drifted shut only a few minutes later, and I fell sound asleep in the safety of his arms.

## 10

RACER

Another race. Another win. Another chance to draw out the motherfucker responsible for the destruction happening around us.

Over the past two weeks, if I wasn't racing, I was working the circuit with Kane. Getting to know the owners of the other teams, we felt out which ones we thought would be allies when the time came to sabotage Franklin's operation. And I spent a fair amount of time trying to fuck my baby into Emily so she was permanently tied to me. There hadn't been a single condom between us since that first night I got inside her sweet pussy.

Tonight had been more telling than usual. During the race, two of the drivers were clearing the track by running other cars off the road or clipping them at just the right angle to cause them to spin out. They were acting like blockers protecting their quarterback—one of Dion Cavern's racers. We already knew he was so fucking crooked I didn't know how he walked straight. But Kane's money guy, Tyre, had been monitoring his bets, and we'd seen him getting chummy with Franklin.

Then the two offensive players had fallen behind Cavern's guy just seconds before the finish line. They'd done a good job making it look natural, as though the quarterback had simply outmaneuvered them and got a burst of speed. I'd bided my time, letting them think they were keeping me in line with their bullshit. Then when they were trying to set up the win, I did my thing—crossing the finish line with a flourish. And damn, it was pretty.

All three drivers had glared at me with murder in their eyes. But when Cavern stepped out of the pit and started screaming at them, they cowered and looked around with fear.

The crowd was dispersing, voices echoing off the concrete walls in the parking lot as I wiped my hands on a rag and walked toward the back of the parking lot, where one of the crew had parked the Chevelle after my heat.

Edge had taken Emily back to her place to grab more of her stuff. I'd pretty much moved her in with me, though I wasn't sure if she'd realized it yet. She'd looked back at me when she slid into Edge's '66 Shelby Cobra, as if she didn't want to leave, and something about that fucking look settled too deep in my chest. I wasn't used to soft glances or needing someone close just to breathe easier. But without her, I felt like I was always seconds away from unraveling.

I climbed behind the wheel of the Chevelle and was just about to turn the key when I caught movement out of the corner of my eye. Two big fuckers peeled away from the shadows at the end of the lot, heads low and shoulders squared.

*Shit.* I was in no mood to put up with these jackasses.

These were the same pricks who'd cornered Emily in the pit. Dez Franklin's muscle—enforcers who'd been around since their boss was just a low-end bookie snapping kneecaps over two-hundred-dollar bets. Now that he ran a whole fucking crew, Dez seemed to think that made him untouchable.

I slid out of the car and leaned against the door casually, as though I didn't feel the shift in the air. Like I wasn't already prepped to whip out my gun from the holster or the spring-loaded blade I kept tucked in my waistband.

"You boys lost?" I asked, keeping my tone even. Not friendly, not hostile, just calm enough to be unsettling.

The taller one smirked like a cocky asshole who truly believed he could intimidate me.

*Fucking morons.*

"Just thought we'd offer a little friendly advice," he sneered.

"Friendly?" I raised a brow. "Sure you fuckers know what that word means?"

The shorter, stocky one spit on the pavement and stepped closer. "Throw the next race."

I chuckled. Couldn't help it. The fucking balls on these guys. "That your advice?"

"Yeah," the tall one said, stepping beside him now. "You've been drawing too much attention. Winning too much. You keep that up, and the wrong people are gonna get real twitchy. We've got the winners picked, and you ain't one of 'em."

"I'll sleep better knowing Dez Franklin's crew is worried about my lap times," I said, pushing off the car with a lazy stretch. "Tell your boss I don't take requests."

"Should reconsider," the stocky one muttered.

"You don't wanna end up like the last guy who said no."

Something in his voice changed. He sounded a little too satisfied and oddly specific.

Something crawled up my spine, and every part of me stilled.

"Yeah?" I tilted my head. "And who was that?"

He grinned, showing off stained and crooked teeth. "Pretty boy driver. Probably would've been a star. But he thought he could play hero, and now he's gonna wake up in the ICU." He snickered, and my trigger finger twitched. "If he wakes up at all."

*Son of a fucking bitch.*

They were talking about Axle.

I straightened to my full height, which was a few inches taller than either of them. Then I took a slow step forward, keeping a tight rein on my rage, only letting them see a hint of it in my eyes.

"You just made a hell of a mistake," I said, my voice dark and deadly.

Both of them looked confused as I closed the distance and got in their faces, my expression flat and lethal, gun in hand, hanging at my side.

"Made one hell of a screwup, boy," I grunted. "Now I know for sure who the fuck put my woman's brother in that coma." Shaking my head in mock disappointment, I casually racked the slide on my Glock. "Rookie move with a death wish."

They tensed, their eyes sliding down to the barrel glinting in the moonlight. I let the silence stretch just long enough for them to feel the threat coiling around every word. Then I shrugged and muttered, "You assholes aren't worth the cleanup," before I pointed my gun at the tall one. Mentally grinning, I used the mag release, chuckling when he dropped his shoulders in visible relief. I racked the slide again, and the bullet in the chamber popped into my hand before I pulled the slide one more time. Then I turned and got into the car, flashing a grin as I cranked the engine.

"Tell your boss I'll be real disappointed if he doesn't come himself next time," I called over the roar of the Chevelle. "Been a while since I put someone in the dirt for fun." I turned up the AC and smirked as I wiped sweat from my brow. "Suppose there are a couple of benefits to living in this fiery level of hell. Alligators make disappearing a body a lot more interesting."

I peeled out and left them standing in a cloud of dust and burnt rubber. By the time I got back to the garage, my jaw was tight enough to crack and my pulse was thundering. The need to cause someone soul-deep pain vibrated through my body.

Only one person was gonna be able to give me peace. I needed to get back to the clubhouse. I needed my woman.

The only thing that had kept me from turning those two bastards into pavement stains was knowing she was safe and waiting for me.

I swapped the Chevelle for my Harley, then gunned the engine and let the wind cut through the heat like a blade.

When I rolled up, the compound buzzed with post-race energy. Inside, the lounge was packed with Redline Kings watching the earlier broadcast of the NHRA Pro Stock Motorcycle race on the big screen.

Kane was sprawled on one of the leather couches, a beer in hand and his boots on the table. His arm was around Emily, who was curled up beside him with a bowl of popcorn in her lap, a faint smile playing on her lips.

My hand nearly went for my gun again, but I reminded myself that Kane and Edge saw her as a sister. It didn't help much, just enough to keep me from putting him in a closed casket.

I walked over to them and growled, "Unless you can ride without hands, take them off my woman."

Kane smirked but removed his arm.

Emily's eyes found mine, and her smile faltered as if she could feel the storm rolling off me and knew I needed her. She stood, handed Edge the popcorn, and crossed to me without hesitation. No questions. Just trust. *Damn, I fucking loved her.*

I took her hand and led her down the hall, straight to our room. Once inside, I kicked the door shut behind us and sat on the edge of the bed before tugging her onto my lap.

She came easily, her legs straddling mine, and her hands resting lightly on my chest.

"What happened?" she asked softly.

Just the sound of her voice calmed the turmoil inside me. I wrapped my arms around her waist and rested my chin on her shoulder, taking a breath before I told her about the two assholes in the parking lot.

Then I paused, dreading what I had to say next.

"Jude?"

"They admitted to putting Axle in the hospital."

Emily's body stiffened in my arms, and her fingers clenched in the fabric of my shirt.

"They did that to him?" Her voice cracked.

"Yeah," I said gently, brushing loose strands of hair away from her face. "Your brother stood up to them. Told 'em to fuck off. So they made an example out of him."

"I knew it," she murmured. "I knew he didn't make a mistake on the track."

"Never doubted it. But now you know for sure."

She sucked in a shaky breath, closing her eyes as she tried to process it. "Why didn't he tell me?"

I rubbed slow circles along her back, grounding her like she did for me. "Because he's your big brother, angel. And no matter how badass he knows you are, he's still gonna want to protect you."

Her shoulders dropped slightly, and when I kissed her forehead, she let out a sigh that sounded like she'd been holding her breath for days.

"I should've checked the car more thoroughly," she whispered, finally opening her eyes and looking into mine. The sadness and guilt filling them sent something sharp through my chest.

"No," I said firmly. "Don't take the blame for that shit. Those bastards got someone good to do their dirty work. Professional. No way did those jackasses do this on their own. And you were working off no fucking intel. You didn't miss something, angel. They buried it deep. We still don't even know exactly what they did. Or even when."

Without the telemetry data and footage, I wasn't sure we ever would.

Emily nodded slowly, but I could still see the guilt lingering in her eyes before she laid her head on my shoulder. I didn't push. I'd help her get there eventually. And when she did, I'd still be right beside her.

THE NEXT NIGHT, the air was thick and electric as I lined up for another qualifier. The crowd was rowdy, adrenaline pumping in my veins, and knowing the bets were heavy on one of Dez Franklin's star drivers, I made a fucking show of it.

Burnout at the start, extra wide turns, and tail-whipping my rival so hard his spoiler clipped the fence. I crossed the finish line three car lengths ahead of the pack, then spun the car in a perfect victory donut before sliding it to a stop with the nose pointed directly at his team box.

Yeah, I was asking for it, and I wanted them to fucking *know* it.

Afterward, Emily went back to the garage with the rest of the pit crew. Kane, Edge, and Nitro—the Redline Kings' sergeant at arms—stayed back to help clear out the stragglers before closing up the gates around another of Kane's makeshift tracks.

I was anxious to get back to my girl, so I left them talking by the betting stands and headed out. Just as I was crossing the parking lot to my bike, I saw the same two dumbass thugs and sighed. I was getting real sick of their ugly faces.

But this time, they brought three more guys as backup.

I smiled as they surrounded me, but with a sinister edge. "Real flattered you felt you needed to bring extra playmates to the sandbox."

"We warned you," the tall one said. "You need to fucking back off."

"Or what?" I asked, tilting my head. "You planning to do more than run your mouth this time? 'Cause I don't bruise easy, but I'm real fuckin' good at breaking things."

That seemed to piss them off, which made me smile.

Stocky moved first. He stepped forward and took a swing. I ducked easily, then broke his nose with the heel of my hand. One of the newbies started to move toward me, but then a low rumble of bikes cut through the night.

Five Redline Kings came roaring around the back lot, led by Kane, all of them grinning.

The gang of meatheads hesitated, looking at each other for direction. When none of them stepped up to lead, they all backed off, but not without one last warning.

"This ain't over."

I smiled and climbed onto my hog. "Nah. It's just starting."

Later, I called Fox. "Gonna need backup, Prez."

He didn't hesitate. "On our way."

I'd known he would agree without question. MCs were chosen family, a bond stronger than blood.

At the garage, Emily was pacing near my office, worry written all over her face. The second she saw me, she blew out a breath and walked straight into my arms, holding me tight.

I gave her the rundown of what happened, and she stared at me like her heart was trying to claw out of her chest.

"Jude." Her brow furrowed, and she shook her head. "This is getting dangerous. You can't just—"

"Hey, hey. Relax, angel." I cupped her face in my hands. "This is what I'm here for. We're not losing. We're setting the trap."

"But what...what if something happens to you?" Her blue eyes filled with tears, and she blinked rapidly, trying to keep them from falling.

I kissed her forehead, her nose, and then her mouth. "Nothing's gonna happen to me."

"You can't know that for sure," she disagreed with a quiet sniff.

"I sure as hell can," I scoffed.

Her nose wrinkled adorably, showing that she might not believe me but was hoping I had an answer that would reassure her. "How?"

I brushed my lips over hers, then locked our eyes. "Because I have something to live for."

She softened, swallowed hard, then nodded. "Me too."

"Come for a ride with me?" I asked.

"Best idea you've ever had," she sighed.

I grinned as I took out my extra helmet and plopped it on her head. "Nah, best idea I ever had was getting inside you."

Emily blushed as her laughter tinkled in the night air, sending warmth through my chest. Yeah, I had *everything* to live for.

We rode through the cool night air, the wind cutting through the weight of the past two days. Her arms around me, body pressed to my back, brought peace and contentment.

Once we got back to the compound, we hopped in the shower to wash away the dust and grime. She sighed and melted against me as hot water streamed down our bodies. When I kissed her, her mouth was soft and as hungry as mine.

I carried her to bed, not giving a single fuck that we were naked and dripping wet.

We held nothing back from each other.

She was mine, and I was hers.

We'd need to keep our cool in the coming fight.

But tonight, we fucking burned.

## 11

### EMILY

The low hum of a phone buzzing on the nightstand pulled me from sleep. I stirred against the warm weight of Jude's body, blinking as sunlight filtered through the blinds. His arms were wrapped tightly around me, one hand resting low on my hip.

I wasn't in a hurry to move, but then it buzzed again, and he reached across me and grabbed it. He squinted at the screen, the faint lines around his mouth tightening.

"Kane," he muttered.

That pulled me a little more awake. "Everything okay?"

Jude didn't answer right away. His thumb tapped out a quick reply, then he tossed the phone onto the mattress with a sigh and rubbed a hand over his jaw, the stubble rasping beneath his fingers.

"What'd he say?"

"He wants us in his office." Jude's gaze met mine. "Said to bring you."

My pulse kicked up. "Why?"

"Didn't say." He gave me a kiss before climbing out of bed, grabbing his jeans, and tugging them on. "But after last night, I'm guessing it's not just a friendly check-in."

I sat up slowly, the sheet pooling around my waist. "You think it's about the sabotage?"

"That or maybe Deviant found something." He tossed me one of his shirts, and I didn't hesitate to pull it on. I liked wearing them because they carried his scent, but Jude preferred me in them because they hid what he considered his. "Either way, we'll know soon."

Based on what Jude had told me, the Iron Rogues' hacker could dig up anything if given enough time. So I wouldn't be surprised if his guess turned out to be correct.

Once we were dressed, Jude moved to the door and glanced back at me. "You good?"

I nodded. "Yeah. Just a little nervous."

He crossed the room in two strides, leaning down

to press a quick, firm kiss to my lips. "Don't be. Whatever's coming, we'll face it together."

I might've only known him for a few weeks, but I didn't doubt his sincerity. Without him, I probably would've fallen apart over Mason still being in a coma. But finding love under the worst circumstances gave me hope. Even though I hadn't actually said those three little words to him yet.

Kane's office wasn't fancy, especially considering he'd tipped into the billionaire range last year. But it had presence, same as the man behind the desk. Calm on the surface, dangerous underneath.

Jude and I stepped inside, and Kane gestured for us to sit, wasting no time as he folded his arms over his chest. "Deviant's been tracking the serial numbers from the tampered components. Turns out the same altered parts show up in multiple rigs. Different builds, different teams, all tied to underground circuits."

Jude's jaw flexed beside me. "Coordinated."

"Exactly." Kane nodded. "The shipments were routed through a shell distributor. On the surface, everything looks clean. But we followed the money. The supplier's a front with a silent partner behind it."

I'd suspected something big, but this sounded like it was on another level.

I leaned forward slightly. "Who?"

Kane's expression turned to granite. "Dez Franklin."

After what Jude told me about the guys who'd threatened him, I wasn't exactly surprised. But hearing our suspicions confirmed still knocked the air out of me.

"He has his hands in more than just the betting rings," Kane continued. "He's part owner in at least three of the underground teams we've been watching. All the ones that have had 'technical issues' at just the right time. Or suddenly surged to win after a competitor dropped out."

Jude didn't say a word, but the tension in his frame was almost tangible.

A knock on the door interrupted the moment, and Kane called out, "Yeah?"

The door opened, and Jax stepped in. He was the Redline Kings version of Deviant, maybe not quite at the same level—unless Kane and Mason had been keeping secrets about his skills. Which wouldn't shock me, considering this was the first time I had been included in club business, thanks to Jude.

"Got it," he announced, eyes lit with triumph. "I

finally cracked the encrypted ledger from the betting syndicate about ten minutes ago. The teams backed by the kingpin all exhibit abnormal win-loss ratios, often tied to suspicious crashes or sudden performance shifts. We're talking race after race."

"Throwing them and rigging results," Jude muttered, a muscle jumping in his jaw.

"And profiting off every damn one," Jax added. "But now we have names, data, and patterns. Enough to make them sweat."

Kane gave a grim nod. "We finally know who's dirty and who we're going to burn down."

Jude smirked. "And which team owners we can approach with a plan."

He sounded so sure, so in control. It made me want to crawl into his lap and never leave.

I snorted at the totally inappropriate thought that maybe then I'd finally learn what promise he'd made to Kane. All three men looked at me, and I pressed my lips together as I waved off their concern.

"Sorry. Just looking forward to making these guys pay so Mason doesn't wake up wondering what we've been doing all these weeks."

None of them looked convinced I was really okay. Jude flung his arm over the back of my chair, and Kane's eyes narrowed slightly. His expression shifted, making him less like a club president and more like a protective pseudo big brother.

Jax sat down and waited to see what happened next.

"There's more," Kane said quietly.

Jude's arm brushed my shoulders as he straightened. I didn't look at him. I couldn't. Not when my gut told me that this wasn't going to be about strategy or takedowns. Or even revenge.

He needed to tell me something about Mason.

Kane glanced at Jax, who gave a small nod and mumbled something about giving us a minute before backing out of the office.

"Deviant and Jax have been digging into your brother's data logger," Kane told me.

I froze, my stomach doing an unpleasant flip. "I thought it was too damaged."

"It was pretty damn bad," he agreed with a sharp nod. "But Jax and Deviant split the load between them. One took the rig's onboard system, the other tackled the backup telemetry. They worked around the corrupt data and found a sliver of clean entry points."

My breath caught.

"They recovered some of the crash data?" My

voice came out strangled, barely more than a whisper.

Kane nodded again. "Not all of it. But just enough."

Hope flared that I would finally get the answers I wanted. Even though Dez Franklin's guys basically admitted to messing with his car, it wasn't enough for me. I needed the details to wrap my head around what happened to my brother. How they managed to take out the guy I'd always thought of as invincible.

Jude reached over, his fingers interlacing with mine, his grip firm and grounding.

After taking a deep breath, I asked, "What did they find?"

Kane scanned my expression before calling, "Come back in, Jax."

Jax returned with his laptop tucked under his arm. He set it on the desk in front of Jude and me. Flipping it open, he pulled up the file they'd recovered. "We noticed strange ECU behavior in the crash data. The air-fuel ratio suddenly spiked lean at full throttle, right before engine detonation."

I leaned forward to get a closer look at the numbers. "They altered the map to reduce the injector duty cycle under full throttle, which fits with what we found under the hood of his car."

"That'd fuck up the engine for sure," Jude agreed.

"So the engine stalled on that turn, and that's why my brother crashed," I whispered. "But the car ran normally in practice. Mason wouldn't have missed something like this, and neither would I."

"They loaded a kill map and set a map-switching condition they knew he wouldn't hit during practice." Jax tapped the keyboard to split the screen. "It didn't change over until he hit 6800 RPM for a full five seconds."

I thought back to the night Mason crashed. "Probably during the first straight when he went full throttle."

Jude whistled. "He must be a hell of a driver to hold it together that long with this kind of sabotage in his ECU."

I sniffled. "The best."

Jude sent me a sideways look but didn't argue.

"He drove like a motherfucking champ." Kane jerked his chin toward the laptop. "They also tampered with the data feedback loop. Fed false data to the dashboard to mask the damage. The Mustang thought it was fine, so Axle got no warning until it was too damn late."

Jude exhaled slowly, shaking his head. "By the

time he noticed the late braking, bad shift timing, and oversteering, it was already too late."

"Not only was the crash not Axle's fault...but his skills at the wheel probably prevented anyone else from getting hurt," Kane pointed out.

I slumped against Jude's side, relief coursing through my veins.

Kane studied me in silence, then pushed back from the desk and circled to my side. "Deviant also recovered some of the video feed. It's shaky and fragmented. But enough to see what happened from Axle's perspective."

My breath caught in my throat.

"Do you want to see it?" Kane asked.

Jude's hand tightened on mine.

I forced myself to meet Kane's gaze. "Yeah. I need to see what he saw."

Jax clicked the file and hit play. The screen flickered once, then stabilized, displaying the split feed: forward camera and dash telemetry. My breath caught when the view from the front of Mason's Mustang filled the frame, tearing around the first curve with familiar grace.

He was so smooth behind the wheel. Confident. In control.

RPMs climbed. The engine roared. The

telemetry numbers stayed in perfect rhythm. There was no warning before everything went to hell. The dash readings remained normal, but Mason swore, "What the fuck?"

Then the Mustang's front end twitched as if the car had suddenly gone light. Mason fought it, but the car veered, the tires catching just enough to yank the whole frame sideways.

My hand flew to my mouth as the video spiraled. The camera jolted as the car spun, metal screeching. For a split second, I could hear Mason yell. Then the feed cut to static upon impact.

The room was silent.

I sat frozen, my lungs refusing to work, tears slipping free as the stillness stretched. Kane shut the laptop without a word, his mouth drawn tight.

Jude didn't say anything. He just stood and gently lifted me into his arms as though I weighed nothing. My fingers curled into his shirt as I buried my face in his chest.

The hallway blurred past us.

He didn't stop until we were back in his room— or ours since I'd stayed in it almost as long as he had. He eased us both down onto the bed without letting go. His back hit the pillows first, and I followed, curled up in his lap as the dam broke.

Sobs tore out of me, harsh and ragged, weeks of fear and guilt pouring out all at once. Jude held me tighter. One hand cradled the back of my head, and the other wrapped securely around my waist, grounding me.

He didn't speak. Didn't try to fix it.

Just held me.

And that was everything.

Long minutes passed before I could form a coherent thought.

My voice cracked on the whisper. "He wasn't at fault. It wasn't his fault. Or mine. And now I finally have proof."

Jude's arms tightened.

And for the first time since that awful night, I felt like I could breathe.

## 12

---

### RACER

The heat rolled heavily through the open bays of Kane's garage, but it didn't hit me as hard as it had when I first arrived. I was surrounded by motorcycles and cars, tools that felt like extensions of my arms, and the sharp scents of motor oil, scorched rubber, and a lingering bite of race fuel.

Other than when I was buried inside my woman, this was where I found the most peace.

I crouched in front of my new Charger—a '69 Daytona. The only thing sexier than this girl was Emily.

Two weeks ago, I'd heard a whisper about it being up for grabs. I didn't even have to think about it. Just wired the cash.

Now she sat in front of me, a 426 Hemi under

the hood, and hell stitched into every inch of her. Her matte-black frame looked like burned charcoal. She had redline pinstriping tracing the body curves, thin as a knife's edge. Black chrome tailpipes, matte graphite wheels, and the interior was blood-red leather with black diamond stitching.

The pointed nose cone, that wicked rear wing, and the low-slung body—she was sin on wheels. Built to own the fucking road and leave everyone choking on its exhaust. It was the kind of machine that didn't just roll in— she announced herself. Deadly, distinctive, and intimidating the hell out of everyone watching.

I couldn't wait to get her out on the road again, but I was also planning to test the sturdiness of the frame by having my woman bouncing on my cock in the back seat.

*Head out of the gutter and into the game, man.*

Thankfully, I was kneeling in front of the Charger where the growing bulge in my pants wouldn't be obvious. Discreetly, I adjusted myself before turning my attention back to the task at hand.

Emily dropped to her heels beside me, her fingers tracing along the fuel lines as she spoke under her breath, more to herself than to me. "Pressure's clean. No inconsistencies."

Her blond hair was yanked up into a messy knot as usual, but she had a pencil tucked through the locks, making it look as though she'd just walked out of a sexy librarian fantasy. Even the cute smear of grease across her cheek made my brain short-circuit. She belonged here—this garage was basically her kingdom—and it drove home how fucking perfect she was for me.

She wore low-slung jeans and one of my racing shirts, knotted at her side to keep it from swallowing her whole. I should've been thinking about sabotage. The race ahead. The plan. But all I could focus on was how the cotton had thinned out across her chest and my name looked right at home stretched over her tits.

*Focus, asshole.*

Outside the shop, the growl of engines echoed, and I got to my feet as five familiar motorcycles rolled in.

Fox swung off his bike first, composed and casual in his sleeveless tee and cut, the tattooed script along his forearm flexing as he tossed his helmet into Reaper's hands. "Nice weather. Almost makes me miss Old Bridge."

Reaper snorted, handing the helmet right back. "Miss it when your balls stop sweating."

Midnight just muttered, "You fuckers bitch more than pregnant old ladies," before heading toward the main bay with that cold-eyed calm that meant he was already thinking about bullets and body bags.

Maverick shook his head. "I'd love to see him say shit like that in front of our women."

A rare grin cut across Fox's face. "Dahlia would shove her piercing gun right between his legs."

"At least when he finds a woman, he'd have some pretty jewelry to distract her from the lack of size," Deviant quipped as he dismounted.

Midnight's only response was to raise his hand and flip them off as he continued walking away.

Deviant and Reaper followed, already arguing about code structure for sensor input.

"I'm telling you, if you'd just run the baseline through my tracker before the sweep, it wouldn't have flagged the—"

"It flagged because your system's dumb as shit," Deviant grunted, adjusting his tablet. "Unlike mine, which actually knows what it's doing."

"You two gonna make out or solve the problem?" I called.

"Depends on how fast you fix that shitbox," Reaper deadpanned without looking up. "Heard she's only pretty from a distance."

"Don't be mad 'cause she's prettier than you," I shot back, smirking. "She'll smoke every one of your Frankenstein projects."

Kane's tech guy, Jax, was waiting for Deviant when he entered the garage and immediately peeled off to an empty office, setting up enough tech to probably ping satellites and hack the Vatican. Kane stood with Fox, Maverick, Edge, and Midnight, quiet murmurs already brewing between them.

I turned back to Emily, who was halfway underneath the Charger now, flashlight wedged between her shoulder and cheek.

"Rear mount's clean. No sensor loops," she said, voice echoing from beneath. "We'd be seeing telemetry drift if it'd been tapped."

"Check the secondary fuses," I said, crouching beside her. "Far left. There's usually a kill switch rig there on these older builds."

She slid out long enough to grab the tool I held out for her, cheeks flushed pink and brow furrowed. That little crease between her eyebrows—focused and frustrated—somehow made me want to flip her over and fuck her senseless across the hood. But I kept my damn hands in check. Barely.

"This car's a monster," she muttered. "But she's clean so far."

That was the problem.

I felt it before I saw it. Something itched at the back of my skull, like static crawling under my skin. We'd *planned* for sabotage. Wanted Franklin to rig the car with some coward's trick so we could expose him. Instead, we were coming up empty, which didn't sit right.

"Angel, come on out and let me get under her."

Emily slid back out and quirked her brow. "Pushing me aside for an older woman?"

I laughed and grabbed a fistful of her shirt, pulling her up into a sitting position. "She's got nothing on you, angel." I kissed her hard and fast, then grinned salaciously. "How 'bout I ride you on her hood and prove it?"

Her cheeks flamed pink, and she shoved at my chest with a giggle. "Get to work, grease monkey."

"Yes, ma'am," I said with a snappy salute.

I switched places with her, took her light and glided under the chassis. Since she'd already done a sweep of the obvious places, I started systematically checking every nook and cranny. When I got to the passenger side footwell, I almost missed it and moved on. But that same itch warned me to take a closer look.

"Wait a second," I said softly.

"What is it?" Her voice was anxious.

"There's something tucked behind the firewall insulation. It's not wired into the usual harness."

*What the fuck?*

I carefully removed the unfamiliar object, then eased out slowly. Cradled in my palm was a small black box the size of a cigarette pack. Flat. Seamless. Way too clean. Shit.

"Get Kane."

By the time I set the device on the workbench and cracked it open with a flathead, Kane, Fox, and the rest were already crowding around. Midnight and Edge flanked Emily instantly, keeping her half shielded with their bodies.

The second I pulled the casing apart, my blood went cold. And from the muttered string of curses behind me, I knew Fox recognized it too.

"Fucking hell. That's a pressure detonator."

"Remote backup too," I muttered, tilting it. "And a fail-safe tied to the engine's RPM. If I'd redlined past six-five, it would've cooked us both."

Emily's breath hitched, and I turned to look at her.

Her lips had gone pale, and one of her hands was gripping Edge's forearm without even realizing it. But unsurprisingly, her chin didn't drop. She didn't so much as fucking flinch. She just stared at that trigger as though she thought she could destroy it with her will alone.

*Mine.*

Possessiveness grew inside me. There was pride in her strength, but mostly, I was ready to rip apart anyone who was a threat to what we were building. My hands were shaking with rage.

Kane looked like he was ready to kill.

"That's not sabotage," he seethed. "That's fucking execution."

I crossed my arms. "We wanted proof. Now we've got enough to burn Franklin and his whole operation to ash."

"Do it," Kane growled. "Shut it the fuck down."

Maverick clapped a hand on my shoulder. "You've got the green light. Go full scorched earth."

Everyone except Edge, Midnight, and Reaper peeled off to start making calls—organizing a meeting with the clean owners and preparing to circulate the evidence.

Meanwhile, I paced, my mind sorting through everything and weeding out the noise so I could focus on what needed to happen next.

Emily sat on the workbench and watched me silently. Her trust and quiet strength were the only things keeping me from losing my shit and going feral.

Franklin had upped the game. He wasn't aiming for a crash to save him from losing. He wanted to end it all. And in his convoluted mind, he thought taking me out was the key. Probably figured if he couldn't rig the race with subtlety, he'd make a statement. A warning.

Yeah, that wasn't ever gonna happen.

"New plan," I muttered, dragging a palm down my jaw. "We hit every one of Franklin's teams. One by one. Sabotage their rides. Screw their odds. Blow their standings. Not literally," I added, glancing at Emily's surprised expression. "Just fuck 'em up enough to wreck their wins."

Reaper looked at Edge. "Get us a list of rigs, and we'll play musical parts."

Deviant and Jax stalked over, their expressions telling me they'd been briefed on the situation. I explained the new plan, and Deviant grinned darkly. "I can spoof tuning data that'll fry their performance without leaving a trail."

Emily rose to her feet, stepped in close, her hand on my arm. "Let me help."

I shook my head. "No."

Her glare could've sliced paint off steel. "Jude—"

"I said no!" My voice came out harsher than I meant it. But just the idea of her being anywhere near those motherfuckers nearly had my head exploding. "This time, it's not just code or sockets. It's breaking and entering. Disabling security. Possibly dropping a few assholes who get in the way. You're not going."

She crossed her arms, toe tapping, chin lifted. "It'll go faster with one more person. And I know those garage layouts. I know where the parts are kept. I've worked beside half of those crews."

I stepped into her space, fisted the front of my shirt where it hung on her body. "And if someone puts a hand on you?" I growled, the angry beast inside me rising, ready to decimate anyone or anything that could hurt my angel.

Her mouth opened, then closed. I watched her struggle, pride and fury at war in her beautiful face. Finally, she gritted out, "What if I take one of your guys with me? They won't let anything happen."

I still hated the idea of her in any proximity to danger, but she'd managed to box me in a corner. If I didn't let her have her way, it would imply that I didn't have faith in my brothers.

*Fuck.*

I glanced at Midnight, and he lifted a brow. "You trust me with your bike. Trust me with your girl."

My eyes moved to Maverick.

He held up his hand. "Swear on my patch, man. She won't so much as get a scratch."

It fucking burned, but I nodded.

"Fine," I growled. "But if one hair on her head gets touched—"

"Then you'll paint the walls with someone's insides," Emily cut in. "Yeah, we know."

My heart stuttered as I looked down at her. At the fierce light in her blue eyes, the set of her jaw, the curve of her perfect lips. My little mechanic angel. She was my heaven on earth, and if I lost her, I'd drag the whole world down to hell.

I lowered my head until my mouth brushed her ear. "When this is over, I'm gonna claim your body. Inch by inch. Remind you who you belong to until you can't fucking walk."

She shivered, then blushed. And I was back to balancing on a wire between protectiveness and raw, filthy hunger.

I kissed her hard, then turned to face my brothers.

"Go suit up," I rasped. "We roll in one hour."

Emily took my hand and gave it a brief squeeze

before walking away with a sway in her hips that made my fists clench.

Fox stepped up beside me, voice low. "You good?"

"Not even close."

"That's love."

I stared at Emily disappearing into the locker room. "No. That's obsession."

Fox snorted. "Can't argue with that."

## 13

### RACER

Every corner of the garage hummed with tension and quiet purpose. We were gathered in Kane's office the night before the Helline Circuit. Reaper leaned against the windowsill with his arms crossed, that wild glint in his eye that usually meant something was about to burn. Midnight sat in the corner, half shadowed, tapping something into his phone. I wouldn't be surprised if he was compiling a kill list. Kane paced behind his desk like a caged panther. Fox, Maverick, and Nitro took up the couch and chairs, all of them looking as though they were ready for war.

We were seven predators circling one shared kill.

Kane stopped walking and braced his fingers on the edge of his desk, dark eyes steady. "Everything's set. Franklin thinks your Charger's rigged to blow. He hasn't laid down a single bet on you." His voice was low and deliberate. "Which means he's going to lose everything when you cross that finish line."

Maverick snorted. "Dumb fuck. We're gonna bury his career in a shallow grave."

"Already got the shovel," Reaper murmured, tossing a spanner from hand to hand like it was a weapon.

"Think he'll piss himself when the odds flip?" Nitro smirked.

"I'm hoping he cries." Edge grinned. "Easier to slit a man's throat when he's already choking on it."

Maverick raised a brow. "Damn, you feeling sentimental tonight?"

Kane leaned back against the wall, arms folded. "He's feeling murderous. We all are."

I clenched my jaw, already picturing Franklin's face when he realized he'd been outplayed. The smug, greasy bastard thought he had it all sewn up. That my Charger would blow sky-high, taking me and his problem with it. He didn't know he was the one sitting on a powder keg.

"All our team owners are in?" I asked.

Kane nodded. "Every single one. They're throwing the race on command. Their drivers know the plan and signals. They'll box you in, block the crash plays, and make damn sure you cross that finish line. Your only job is to stay alive and win."

Fox leaned back, calm and collected in a way that meant he was at his deadliest. "Bets'll go down at the last possible second—big, loud, and all on you."

I cracked my neck and let my gaze slide over all of them. "So Franklin gets nothing. His boys lose. His odds go up in flames, and his backers get burned with him."

"That's the goal." Nitro's grin didn't reach his eyes. "And if it all goes to shit, we improvise."

We discussed things for a few more minutes, then the meeting concluded.

"Hey," Fox called, nodding me into the hallway. "Got something for you."

We walked a few feet away before he handed over a plastic-wrapped bundle and clapped me on the back. "Thought you might need this."

I peeled the wrap away, and my chest squeezed.

Emily's property vest.

Black leather, soft and supple, sized for her frame. Her name was stitched on the front left breast in silver thread, clean and feminine. But it was the back that hit hardest—the Iron Rogues patch, bold as hell and Property of Racer stitched in bone-white thread across the center.

*Fuck.*

My mouth dried out, and a lump caught in my throat that I'd never admit to having. Not even under torture.

"Fox—" I started.

"Don't say it," he muttered, grin stretching. "I remember your bullshit speech. Still think you're too smart to fall?"

I looked up and shot him a glare.

He laughed. "Yeah, yeah. That's what I thought. So smart you're carrying around that crazy-eyed look Maverick had when Molly told him she was late."

"Fuck off."

He just chuckled and walked off, tossing one last look over his shoulder. "She's yours. Let everyone know it."

Everyone would fucking know it. My fingers slid over the leather, the stitching, the claim.

*Mine.*

I gripped the vest tighter and started toward the office Kane had given me when I first arrived. When I got there, I turned toward the big window just as movement flickered in the corner of my eye.

Through the big glass pane that overlooked the adjacent bay, I saw her.

Every other thought vanished.

She stood just inside the open rolling door of the private work area. Her blond hair was twisted up, a few tendrils curling down around her neck. The moonlight spilled across her skin like liquid silver, casting her in a soft glow, outlining every curve beneath the tight tank top she wore—low and clinging to her tits. Her cutoffs hugged her hips like a second skin. Her long legs were bare, golden from the sun, gleaming faintly in the garage lights.

And she was talking to Gauge.

Motherfucker was standing too close. Too casual. His posture relaxed in that easy way that made my knuckles itch.

My pulse turned into a snarl, and my vision tinted red.

I dropped the vest on the desk and stalked out of the office without a word, each step deliberate, lethal, burning with cold fury. My boots echoed on the concrete floor, but neither of them turned until I slammed my palm against the metal bay door control. The sound echoed like a gunshot, and both of them flinched as the door rolled down behind me with a metallic rattle and a heavy thud, cutting us off from the rest of the garage.

Gauge started to speak, but I didn't give him the chance.

"You have five seconds to walk away," I growled, my voice low and flat.

He looked between us, eyebrows lifting, but he wasn't stupid. One look at my face, and he backed off, raising both hands as if I were ready to shoot him.

Because I was holding a fucking gun on him.

He hesitated, then wisely decided he didn't want to test me. He gave Emily a stiff nod and ducked under the bay door before it fully sealed.

I lowered the gun and set it on a work cart before I turned toward her.

Her arms were crossed, brow lifted, not cowed in the slightest. "That was unnecessary."

As I ate up the distance between us, she took one step back, then another, until her shoulders hit the wall. Her eyes were wide, lips parted, breath caught somewhere between a gasp and a challenge.

"You're practically naked," I rasped, one palm braced beside her head, caging her in. "And letting some other man breathe your air. You think my reaction was unnecessary?"

Her mouth parted in indignation. "Naked? Are you kidding me?"

"You're not wearing a fucking bra."

"It's built in!"

"Don't give a fuck," I growled. "Easy access."

Then I yanked the neckline of her tank down with one hand.

She gasped, eyes wide as her tits bounced free, with no barrier, her nipples were tight from the night air and my fury. That thin built-in shelf didn't mean shit to my brain in this state. My mouth watered. My cock throbbed.

But I wasn't done.

I shoved my other hand down the front of her shorts, fingers sliding past the waistband, straight to her bare, wet pussy. No panties.

I sucked in a breath through my teeth. "No bra. No panties. Talking to another man like that." My fingers curled possessively, stroking her slit. "You trying to kill me, angel?"

"I didn't do it on purpose," she whispered, breath hitching.

"You don't have to," I murmured, dragging my fingers up through her slick folds. "You walk into a room, and I'm fucking gone."

I curled my fingers between her thighs and felt

how wet she already was. "You don't get to dress like this and talk to other men."

"I wasn't doing anything wrong."

"You were tempting fate," I growled, voice low and lethal.

Her tank was still bunched under her tits, and her chest rose and fell with every ragged breath.

"You think I'm just gonna let you walk around like that?" I rasped, as I pressed her back to the cinderblock with one hand. "Dripping for me, uncovered, and letting some other asshole smile at you?"

Her lips parted, but nothing came out except a choked moan when I shoved a finger inside her and slammed my mouth down on hers. The last shred of my control burned away.

I yanked her shorts down with one hand, tearing the button clean off in the process, and she kicked them free as I dropped to my knees. Her thighs parted without hesitation, and I growled as I buried my face between them.

She tasted like heaven and heat and everything that belonged to me.

She jerked. "Oh, oh yes!"

"Mine," I snarled, rising to my feet. I flipped her around, bracing one hand on the wall above her head while the other dragged my zipper down. My cock sprang free, thick and hard, already leaking. "This pussy's mine. Say it."

Emily gasped, her hands flying up to brace herself. "Yours. It's yours."

"That's right, angel."

Grabbing my cock, I groaned as I guided it to her soaked slit. No teasing. No hesitation. I lined myself up with her soaked pussy and slammed inside with one brutal thrust that made her cry out and slap a hand over her mouth.

"Yeah, angel," I gritted, hips pistoning forward again. "Take it. Take what's mine."

She moaned, back arching, pushing herself onto me with a desperation that made my vision blur.

"Fuck, Emily," I rasped against her ear. "You're so tight I can barely move. This pussy was made to keep me buried in it."

"Jude...yes...oh yes!"

I reached up and fisted her hair, yanking her head back just enough to whisper in her ear. "You feel that? That stretch? That fullness?" Another thrust, deep and hard. "That's me. Filling up what's mine."

The walls echoed the sound of skin against skin as I pounded into her, relentless and unhinged. I bent low and bit her shoulder, one hand on her hip, the other gripping one of her tits, pinching and tugging the nipple until her knees buckled and she had to lean against me to stay upright. Then I did the same with the other side until she was shaking with need.

Her pussy clenched tight around me, and I groaned, fucking into her harder.

"I'm gonna fuck you sore," I growled. "You'll feel me tomorrow. You'll feel me every time you sit. Every time you move. Every step you take, you'll remember how I owned this tight little pussy."

She whimpered, her nails scraping the wall, body shuddering with the force of my thrusts. "Jude, oh, yes! Please! Oh!"

"You're not just mine, angel. You're my fucking obsession. Gonna ruin you for anyone else."

She sobbed, clenching around me. Her pussy was like a vise, fluttering and squeezing with every stroke, dragging my release closer with punishing speed.

I reached down and rubbed her clit with rough, possessive strokes. "Come for me. Now. I want you to come while I breed you."

Her whole body tensed.

"You want my come, angel?" I rasped. "You want me to put a baby in you, don't you?"

She moaned so loud, it echoed off the walls. "Yes! Yes, oh my—"

"Gonna fill you, angel. Knock you up so no one ever looks at you without knowing you're mine."

She cried out again, high and keening, shaking around me as her orgasm hit. I didn't slow down. If anything, I fucked her harder, shoving her up the wall with every thrust.

"Such a good girl," I muttered, voice hoarse. "Taking every inch. Greedy little pussy needs to be bred, doesn't it?"

She nodded frantically, lost in it. "Yes! Yes, please—"

That was it. That was the end.

I shoved deep and came with a groan, my whole body tensing as I emptied myself inside her, hot and thick and endless. She shattered around me again, screaming my name, her legs trembling, barely able to stay upright as her pussy milked every last drop.

I stayed there, locked inside her, panting against the back of her neck, chest pressed to her spine. When I could breathe again, I pulled out and spun her around, lifting her into my arms. Her thighs were sticky with my come, her cheeks flushed, lips kiss-swollen, eyes glassy.

*Mine.*

I kissed her slowly this time, full of all the things I didn't know how to say. When I finally set her down, she wobbled, clinging to my arms.

"Can't walk?" I asked, feeling smug.

She glared up at me. "Asshole."

I smirked and pressed my lips to hers. "You're mine."

She looked as though she might say something smart again, so I kissed her again. This time, it was soft and slow, almost reverent. I poured out everything I felt but didn't think she was ready to hear.

When I released her lips, she looked at me, blue eyes wide and wet.

"I was always yours," she whispered.

And fuck me—I felt that down to my bones.

## 14

---

### EMILY

The roar of the crowd filtered through the glass, muffled but impossible to ignore. I paced the length of the Redline Kings owner's box, arms crossed tight against my chest as I stared at the track below. The Helline Circuit was still an underground race, but Kane paid off the right people to be able to host at the Redline Speedway.

I hated being stuck in here.

The pit was where I belonged. Where I could run diagnostics, check telemetry, and shout strategy over the headset. Not locked away in an air-conditioned skybox, watching through reinforced glass as if I were some delicate spectator.

But Jude had put his foot down. Hard. And I hadn't wanted to distract him while he was racing against drivers who literally wanted to kill him. So I'd given in without a fight.

Kane was at my side as the signal dropped. Jude's Charger peeled out with a growl that set my heart racing. The others surged with him, and engines snarled as tires screamed across the pavement.

For the first couple of laps, he held steady. All smooth lines and tactical turns.

Even from up here, I could feel it—the tension coiling beneath the surface.

We were all waiting for Dez's guys to pull some crap on the track. But at least Jude had backup this time from some of the other teams.

"He's driving tight," I murmured.

Kane nodded. "He's waiting."

"For what?"

"For someone to make a move."

As if on cue, one of the cars on his left swerved inward, trying to sideswipe him on the next bend. My stomach dropped.

"Crap," I breathed.

But Jude didn't flinch. He flicked the wheel with terrifying precision and sent the other car spinning into the barricade in a burst of tire smoke and sparks. The crash shook the fence, and the crowd erupted in a roar.

I pressed my fingers to my lips, heart thundering. "That wasn't a fluke."

"Nope," Kane said grimly. "It was a failed ambush."

More cars pushed in, one after the next—testing, feinting, trying to crowd him out. But I saw it. I saw the pattern.

"His backup," I whispered.

A familiar car clipped another that got too close to Jude. A second redirected the heat off him with a deliberate drift. The other teams had come through for us.

The next few laps were brutal.

Every time Jude tried to pull ahead, someone blocked him. One of our allies clipped another driver's tail just long enough to open a gap, but it didn't last.

Then one of Dez's drivers broke through the line.

I saw it coming a split second before it happened —too fast to scream, too slow to stop. The other car slammed into Jude's side with vicious intent, and his Charger spun.

My breath lodged in my throat.

The whole track seemed to tilt as his car whirled, tires screaming, smoke pluming from the pavement. I fisted my hands at my sides, heart pounding against my ribs like it was trying to escape.

*Don't crash. Please, don't crash.*

But Jude didn't lose control. He never did.

With a move so fast it was almost invisible, he corrected the angle, straightened the frame, and hit the gas. The other driver was still recovering when Jude swung wide and plowed into his side with a punishing force.

The crowd roared as the car veered off track and crashed into the barricade.

Jude didn't look back. He shot down the straightaway like a man possessed.

I didn't breathe again until he crossed the finish line. In first place, just as we'd planned. Dez Franklin had fallen into our trap and was now royally screwed. I was thrilled, although a part of me still wanted to see him pay even more for what he'd done to my brother.

The owner's box erupted in cheers behind me, but I barely registered them. All I wanted was to get to Jude.

I whirled toward the door and made it three steps before one of Mason's club brothers and one of Jude's blocked the way.

"Move," I demanded.

"Can't." Blitz shook his head. "Racer said he'd break all our legs if we let you out."

My jaw dropped. "Are you serious?"

"Dead," Maverick replied. "Said he'd start with the knees."

I gaped at them, but Kane didn't even look up from his phone.

"Love you like a sister, Em, but I'm not taking a bullet for you," he muttered. "After what he just pulled off, he's earned the right to be a possessive asshole for five minutes."

I huffed and crossed my arms.

"I can't wait until it's your turn," I growled.

Kane finally looked up and rolled his eyes. "Don't hold your breath while you wait."

I started pacing again, frustration and adrenaline buzzing through every nerve. I wasn't going to be calm until I saw Jude with my own eyes. Then I was going to kill him for scaring me like that. Right after I kissed the hell out of him.

The door slammed open so hard it bounced off the stopper. Jude stalked into the owner's box, helmet in one hand, the other clenched at his side. He was still in full racing gear—sweat-slicked, flushed, and brimming with adrenaline-fueled fury and triumph.

I didn't hesitate.

I launched across the room, running full tilt until I collided with him. His arms caught me mid-sprint, wrapping around my waist and lifting me clean off the ground. Then he spun me once with a sharp exhale, as though he needed proof that I was safe, even though I hadn't been the one in danger.

My legs clung to his hips, my arms locked around his neck, and my face buried in his shoulder. For one perfect second, the world disappeared.

Then I yanked back just enough to glare at him.

"You're not allowed to do that again," I snapped, jabbing a finger against his chest. "My heart can't take it."

His smirk was maddening. "That your way of saying you love me?"

I tried to pout, but it crumpled the second I looked at him.

"Yeah," I muttered, dropping my forehead to his. "I love you, you big jerk."

"Big jerk?" he echoed, his grin widening.

"You totally turned every club brother against me," I complained.

He quirked a brow. "Only because I know you so well. You never would've known if you hadn't tried to leave the owner's box—like I told you not to."

"Whatever," I mumbled, since I couldn't argue with his logic.

Pressing his finger under my chin, he tilted my head up to meet his gaze. His smirk vanished, replaced by something raw and reverent. "I love you too, baby."

Jude showed me how he felt every single day, but hearing those words from him settled something deep inside me. My heart felt full to bursting as his mouth found mine in a kiss that wasn't soft or slow. It was everything that had built between us—weeks of tension, fear, wanting, and relief—all crashing into one moment.

The guys hooted behind us, someone shouting something crude, but I didn't care.

I melted into Jude and celebrated our victory against the monster who put my brother in his hospital bed by kissing the man I loved.

A throat cleared behind us, loud enough to break the spell of the kiss. Jude didn't release me right away, pressing his lips to my forehead before glancing over his shoulder with a growl of irritation.

Fox stood in the doorway, arms crossed and mouth quirked in a half-apologetic, half-amused grin.

"Sorry to interrupt the lovefest," he drawled. "But we have club business. Need you, Racer."

Jude's jaw flexed. He looked back at me, eyes dark with something fierce and unreadable, and cupped my cheek in one gloved hand.

"I gotta go for a bit," he said, voice low and rough. "I'll meet you at the Redline Kings clubhouse when this is done."

I nodded, trying to hold back the disappointment that flared in my chest. This was how MCs worked. I knew that. Even respected it. But I wasn't happy about the timing of his president's request.

Jude leaned in and kissed me again, slower this time. Then he released me, brushing his thumb over my bottom lip before stepping back.

Fox gave me a chin lift before disappearing down the hall.

I stayed where I was, watching Jude walk away. I had his heart. I knew that much.

But maybe I wanted more.

Maybe I wanted the words stitched on leather that would make it official. His old lady. His *everything*.

## 15

---

### RACER

They didn't beg when we snatched them off the street.

But then, I never gave them the chance.

Dez Franklin and his two pit bulls just sat in silent arrogance, even when we had them bound, gagged, and covered in hoods in the back of the transport van.

The Redline Kings didn't waste time. After the race, Kane gave a single nod, and that was all it took. The three men were yanked off the asphalt and tossed into a cage on wheels. Then we drove them straight to hell.

Two levels beneath the Redline Kings' garage was the hidden underbelly that Edge had mentioned, but few ever got to see. Like the garage bays, the rooms were reinforced concrete, industrial-grade steel, and had tile floors that were easy to clean. But down here, there was also a security system that could rival any federal lockup. No cell signal. No cameras. No chance of anyone screaming loud enough for the outside world to hear.

This wasn't a place for mercy. It was for monsters to meet the men who hunted them.

The door thudded shut behind us as I followed Kane, Edge, and Nitro down the stairs. With each step, the air grew cooler, but remained damp from the humidity, causing the walls to sweat with condensation. The faint scent of bleach lingered in the air.

The Iron Rogues, the Redline Kings, Hounds of Hellfire...we all had blood on our hands. We were outlaw clubs. Not fucking choirboys. The world liked black and white, but we lived in gray. The place no one without a patch ever wanted to admit was necessary to humanity. Some of us leaned closer to the shadows than others, but there were always lines. Limits. A code. And when that code was broken—when someone fucked with our people— that was when the hunters got unleashed.

And tonight, I was the executioner.

Franklin and his boys weren't in the cells for

slinging cheap parts or screwing up a race. They were here because they'd rigged cars to fucking explode, buried drivers in twisted metal, and tried to kill me to cover it up.

And worse—they targeted Emily.

That was what sealed their fate. There'd be no trial. No lawyer. No redemption arc.

Nothing but judgment. They weren't going to rot in some prison. They were going to pay in blood. Drop by drop.

Kane nodded to one of his enforcers, and the door to the first room swung open. Dez sat chained to a steel chair, hood pulled off, wrists cut and bruised from the zip ties we'd replaced with shackles. He looked up at me through one swollen eye, sneering as if he thought he was the smartest guy in the room. His delusions of grandeur would quickly be shattered.

"About time," he grunted. "You wanna get on with your little show so I can get back to my blow and pussy?"

I rolled my shoulders and stepped into the room. His words had no effect on me.

Most of the time, I was a laid-back guy with a ready smile. But here? And in The Room back in Old Bridge? They were the only places that knew this side of me. Calm, solid as the walls, unmovable. I lacked emotion. Only the icy need for justice trickled through my veins.

The fluorescent lighting flickered above me, casting shadows on the walls that were streaked with rust, sweat, and old stains that would never fully fade.

"You seem to misunderstand what's happening here," I deadpanned. "You're here to do penance."

Dez's smirk twitched. "You some kinda priest now?"

"Nope," I murmured, slowly circling his chair. "But I'm the one who's going to make sure no one else ends up in a hospital or a coffin because you got greedy."

"Business is business," he spat. "You're in the game, you know that. Collateral damage happens."

"Business?" I stopped in front of him and knelt so we were eye to eye. "You almost killed my friend. Put my woman's brother in a coma. Had your goons try to scare her off, to run her over with a car. You tried to blow up my car on the track, with her in the pit." I smoothly stood back up and walked toward the stainless-steel table against the back wall that was covered in tools. Despite listing out his sins, I remained detached and unemotional.

"That wasn't business. That was personal. And so is this."

"What the fuck do you want from me?" he snapped.

Once I reached the table, I slid my hand across the row of tools, making them clink together.

"I'm giving you the chance to pay reparations," I told him honestly.

He snickered, then taunted, "You think you can get a fucking dime outta me?"

"I don't want payment in money." My fingers settled on a double-edged, fixed-blade combat knife. Clean. Sharp. I turned around, dagger in hand, and walked back over to him.

When he saw the blade, he swallowed hard. "You–you can't just—"

"I can," I replied. "And after I'm done, I'll sleep just fine."

It didn't take long to get the name of the tech guy who helped him with the digital logs, the one who built the explosive device in my car, and a list of all the crooked racers and team owners he'd worked with.

After that, the pain wasn't about information. Like I told him, it was about penance.

For every driver forced off a track.

For every man who was damaged or broken.

For every man they killed.

And for every drop of fear they instilled in Emily.

I didn't gut him. Didn't turn into a monster and rip him to shreds. This wasn't about splatter and carnage. It was about control. Consequence. And that required precision.

When it was done, with his head lolling to the side and blood seeping from the slash across his neck, I leaned in one last time before the lights went out.

"That was for Axle," I said quietly. "And for every racer you left bleeding in a wreck you caused."

I stood and wiped the blade on his shirt.

"And that was for looking at my woman like she was prey."

Kane stepped into the doorway, his eyes steady. He glanced at Franklin, whose eyes had finally gone blank.

"You done?" he asked.

I nodded.

He jerked his chin up, then tilted his head toward the hallway. "Go on and get cleaned up. Edge will handle the disposal."

I passed him the knife and walked out, not sparing a glance for the two bodies in the other rooms. They were already dead. Edge had seen to that, though it looked like he'd let his crazy side out to play a little.

There was a bathroom at the far end of the corridor, something Kane had installed for this exact reason. It was sterile and tiled in industrial gray, featuring a deep shower stall, a heavy-duty sink, an industrial dishwasher, and a wall-mounted cabinet stocked with cleaning supplies and bandages.

I peeled off my shirt first, tossing it in the bin marked "burn." My cut had stayed outside the room. I never brought that symbol near blood unless it was in a fight worth honoring. And this hadn't even been close to that.

The shower roared on as I stepped inside, letting the near-scalding water sear away the traces of death. Blood swirled in pink ribbons down the drain, and I scrubbed my skin until the water ran clear. But even then, I stayed under the spray for a while longer, letting the heat melt the tension from my stiff muscles.

Slowly, I began to thaw inside as well.

When I emerged, I dried off with a clean towel and pulled on a fresh shirt from a cabinet where they kept extra clothes.

Out in the hallway, it was quiet and still. The men were gone.

Edge would handle the mess. I didn't need to know how.

As I made my way up the stairs, my boots echoed against concrete and steel. With every step, I felt the last of the ice inside me melting away.

It was nearly three in the morning when I arrived back at the clubhouse. The halls were silent except for the low hum of the AC buzzing faintly above me as I made my way to our room. When I opened the door, moonlight spilled in across the floorboards and over the bed.

Emily was curled beneath the blankets, her hair a golden halo against the dark blue sheets and pillow. One arm was tucked beneath her head, the other flung out as though she'd been reaching for me.

I kicked off my boots, stripped out of my clothes, and slid onto the mattress behind her, wrapping my arm around her waist and pulling her close. She stirred when I pressed a kiss to her shoulder, sighing softly before she snuggled in closer.

She was safe. Warm. Alive.

Knowing that the morning would bring a new chapter in my life, I felt free and at peace as I closed my eyes and slept.

THE SMELL of steam and soap filled my nose as I slowly came awake.

I rolled over, muscles sore but loose, and caught the sound of water running from the en suite. The bathroom door was cracked just enough to let in the glow.

A smile slowly crawled across my face as I realized Emily was in the shower.

I reached into the drawer beside the bed and pulled out the little black box I'd tucked there a few days ago—for when we made it through the storm.

Now, all the bullshit was behind us, and I couldn't wait to put my physical claim on Emily so everyone knew she belonged to me. I set the box on the dresser, then completed one more task before stripping and stepping into the bathroom.

She was rinsing shampoo from her hair, eyes closed, face tilted toward the spray. Her body was slick and glistening in the soft light, every soft curve and tight line a siren's call straight to my dick.

I stepped in behind her, wrapping my arms around her waist. She jumped, then relaxed into me instantly.

"You're awake," she whispered. "I'm so glad you're back."

"Me too, angel," I murmured against her neck. "It's over."

Her hands slid over mine. "What do you mean?"

"I mean we're done here. We can go home now."

She turned in my arms, eyes wide and searching. "Home?"

"Yeah, angel," I said, brushing a wet strand from her cheek with a crooked smile. "You're mine. I'm keeping you. Not gonna leave without you. Where I go, you go. Because home is wherever you are."

Her lips parted in a soft gasp, and something melted behind her eyes. She looped her arms around my neck and moved in close until our bodies were practically glued together in the hot spray. Her hard nipples pressed against my chest, and my already hard dick swelled to the point of pain.

"I love you, angel. More than life."

Emily lit up like the fucking Fourth of July.

"I love you," she whispered. "So much it hurts."

I crushed my mouth to hers, my tongue sweeping deep, my hands sliding down to cup her ass. When I rocked my hips toward her, her breath hitched and her knees buckled, but I caught her and backed her up against the tile wall.

"Wanna show me?" I rasped.

She dropped to her knees without hesitation.

My hand gripped her hair as her lips wrapped around my cock, and I groaned as her tongue swirled —hot, slick, and perfect. She took me deep, worshipping every inch until I was on the edge of losing it.

When I yanked her back up, she gasped in surprise.

"Need to be inside you," I growled.

I lifted her by the thighs and drove into her in one hard thrust.

She cried out, grabbing onto my biceps, her fingers digging into my skin as I fucked her against the shower wall.

I didn't take her soft and sweet. It was hot, hard, and primal. A branding.

"Mine," I growled as I exploded inside her.

When we finally emerged, damp and breathless, Emily reached for the clothes she'd laid out, then looked around in confusion. "What the...? Where are my clothes?" Then her eyes landed on the only item on the bed, and she froze.

I leaned against the doorway, towel slung around my hips, smirking. "Try that on instead."

She blinked, still staring at where I'd draped a cut across the bed. Not mine.

Hers.

Slowly, almost reverently, she picked it up. Black leather. Her name stitched over the heart in silver thread. When she turned it around, her breath caught.

She clutched the vest to her chest and spun around to face me with wide eyes. "You...you want me to be your old lady?"

I arched a brow. "You serious?"

Her lips opened, then closed, her eyes filled with hope.

"Angel," I sighed, stepping closer. "I told you I loved you. I've been fucking you bare for weeks trying to breed you. You think I'm not claiming you in every way that matters?"

She swallowed, blinking rapidly as her blue orbs glistened.

"You're mine." My voice was low and fierce as I helped her slip her arms into the vest. "You're gonna be my old lady. My wife. The mother of my kids. The woman I build a life with and grow old beside. And you better believe that comes with more than just a leather vest."

I grabbed the box off the dresser and popped it open. Inside, a diamond ring glittered. Beside it were two simple, platinum matching bands, one a little thicker and more masculine.

Emily gasped, and a heartbeat later, she launched herself into my arms, wrapping her legs around my waist. Then she raised her left hand and wiggled her fingers. *Fuck, she was cute.* I laughed as I slipped the ring onto her finger.

Then I sealed my mouth over hers, and fire blazed between us, burning so fast and hot we almost didn't make it back to the bed before round two.

Later, tangled in the sheets, she held up her hand again, admiring her ring as it sparkled in the light streaming through the cracks in the blinds.

"It's beautiful," she said softly. "And, um, really big."

"You don't like big things?" I teased. "'Cause the way you scream when I'm filling you with my thick cock hints otherwise."

She shoved my shoulder lightly as she giggled. "I just meant, it had to have been really expensive. You didn't have to spend money like that on me, Jude. I would be happy with a piece of string tied around my finger as long as it means I get to marry you."

Smiling, I kissed her tenderly. "You don't have a choice, angel." Then I chuckled. "But I definitely wasn't gonna let my wife walk around without a big-ass statement that you're claimed. It's not as if I can't afford it anyway."

Emily tilted her head. "What?"

"I made a fuck ton of money back when I was racing full-time, and I still take home heavy purses when the mood to hit the track strikes me. With the custom bikes, shit for the club, and helping Kane manage the races in Tennessee, an expensive ring doesn't even make a ding in my bank account."

She leaned up on her elbow and stared at me. "Are you telling me that you're rich?"

"No, I'm telling you *we* are loaded."

"Hmm." Her tone was cryptic.

"Does that bother you?"

After a second, she shook her head while she trailed the tip of one finger down my chest. "Nah. It might make you a little more attractive, though."

I laughed because she was so damn adorable, and I knew that money wasn't something that would ever sway Emily. Her heart was too genuine, but I couldn't help teasing her back. "Whatever it takes to keep your legs open, angel."

She snorted. "As if you have any trouble with that now."

Grinning, I rolled on top of her and ground my hard shaft against her hot pussy. "Prove it."

We were slick with sweat and completely satisfied when I rolled off her and pulled her close, her back snug against my chest. I pressed a kiss to her bare shoulder and murmured, "We should start packing up your place. Once your brother's back on his feet, we'll head to Tennessee."

She stilled for a second. "You're waiting...for Mason?"

"Course I am," I said against her skin. "You wouldn't want to leave while he's in the hospital. And I'm not going anywhere without you."

She buried her face in my chest, and I heard a muffled sniff. "I was going to ask, but you were already planning on it."

"'Cause I love you, angel. I want you to be happy, and I'll do anything in my power to make sure I see that gorgeous smile every day for the rest of our lives. " I grabbed her chin and lifted it so I could see her face. "Fuck that," I growled. "You'll be mine forever."

The sun was high by the time we got out of bed again, stomachs growling loudly enough to compete with the Harleys outside.

We were halfway dressed when my phone buzzed with a text.

EDGE

Turn on the news.

Curious, I grabbed the remote and flipped it to the local channel.

"Breaking news out of Crossbend. Three bodies have been identified in the charred remains of a wrecked SUV. Authorities say the fire was so intense that dental records were required for confirmation."

Photos flickered across the screen. Dez Franklin and his two goons.

I sat down beside Emily and watched in silence as the anchor wrapped the story up.

"Preliminary findings suggest the men were unable to exit the vehicle before it was engulfed in flames. Authorities have not released further details."

Another message buzzed through.

EDGE

Fitting, right? Dying in a fiery crash.

Then a third one.

EDGE

Poetic justice, Redline Kings style.

I chuckled and was about to set my phone down when I noticed yet another text.

MAVERICK

You mean Iron Rogues style,
fucker.

That was when I realized it was a group text. The two of them started bickering about which MC was more badass, and I laughed, putting my phone on silent.

Emily rolled her eyes. "For a bunch of hard-ass bikers, you guys can be so childish sometimes."

Before she knew what hit her, she was on her back with my body hovering over her. "More than willing to prove I'm a man, angel."

"My man," she whispered as she wrapped her legs around my waist.

"Damn straight."

# EPILOGUE
## EMILY

*Three weeks later*

My phone rang just as the sun was starting to rise. My eyes were bleary as I saw the hospital's number flash across the screen.

I answered with a breathless, "Hello?"

I could practically hear the nurse's smile through the phone as she said, "You'll want to come in, Miss Novak. Your brother woke up."

I was already shouting for Jude before the call ended.

Half an hour later, I stood just inside Mason's hospital room, heart pounding as I stared at my big brother. He looked pale and worn, but his eyes were open and alert. *Finally.*

And laser-focused on the man holding my hand.

"Tell me I'm hallucinating," Mason muttered. His voice was gravelly, but the sarcasm still hit home. "Because the last time I checked, I didn't authorize my little sister to hook up with some guy, much less from another club, while I was unconscious."

Jude just squeezed my hand and waited.

I stepped closer to the bed, trying not to cry. "Mase, this is—"

He cut me off with a groan. "Let me guess. 'He's different, Mason. He's sweet and strong and—'" His eyes narrowed. "Does he at least treat you right?"

Jude's low voice rumbled beside me. "Better than anyone else ever could. And I plan to keep treating her right for the rest of her life."

Mason blinked, his gaze darting between us as his brows drew together. "Okay. What the hell happened while I was out? I'm gonna blame it on the coma because I just realized you're wearing his property patch. I was only in a coma for a few weeks, Em. What the fuck?"

A wave of nausea slammed into me so hard I barely got the words out, "Oh no."

I dropped Jude's hand and sprinted for the bathroom. My stomach turned itself inside out while I knelt on the cold tile, hugging the bowl and silently begging the universe to let me breathe.

Jude was at my side before I even started to puke. He pulled my hair back gently and rubbed soothing circles on my back.

When I finally sat back, pale and trembling, I gave him a sheepish look. "That wasn't dramatic timing at all."

He chuckled, brushing a damp strand from my face. "You okay, angel?"

I nodded. "Yeah. I should be good now."

We stepped out of the bathroom to find Kane standing just inside Mason's door, arms crossed, face unreadable.

He glanced at me, then at Jude. "Heard Axle was awake."

I flashed him a sheepish smile. "Sorry, I should've texted."

Kane waved off my concern. "I get it, Em. You were too excited to think of anything but getting to your brother."

Jude shot Kane an apologetic look. "I should've let you know."

My brother's glare sharpened. "Who the hell *are* you?"

"Racer?" Kane jerked his chin toward Jude.

"He's the reason we got the bastards who took you out. The whole damn ring."

I punctuated the last word by lifting my hand to show off the glittering diamond on my finger. "And your future brother-in-law, as soon as you're healthy enough to walk me down the aisle."

Mason opened his mouth, then closed it, at a loss for words for the first time in his life.

"You don't have to like me, Axle," Jude said bluntly. "But you're gonna have to get used to me."

Mason's eyes narrowed. "Excuse me?"

"I'm not leaving," Jude said. "Not without Emily. Or our kid."

You could've heard a damn pin drop.

"What?" Mason barked.

"Our kid?" Kane repeated, one brow raised.

I cleared my throat, cheeks flushing. "Uh...yeah. I just found out. That's what the, um, bathroom detour was about."

Mason groaned and dropped his head back against the pillow. "You're telling me I just woke up from a fucking coma to find out my sister's in love, engaged to a biker, and pregnant?"

I stepped closer to the bed and kissed his temple. "You'll get used to it. He's not so bad once you stop thinking about killing him."

Jude growled low in his throat. "That better not have been your plan."

Kane slapped a hand on Jude's shoulder. "Come on, Romeo. Let's give these two a minute before you end up making more enemies."

With a final squeeze of my waist, Jude followed Kane out of the room.

Mason stared at me, silent for a long moment.

"You really love him?" he finally asked.

"I do," I whispered.

"Then I guess I'd better get better fast." He sighed. "Sounds like I have a fuck ton of big-brother duties to catch up on."

I laughed and squeezed his hand. "Definitely."

# EPILOGUE
## RACER

*Five years later*

The smell of hickory smoke drifted in the breeze, curling through the branches of the big oak tree at the edge of our yard. Sunlight filtered through summer leaves, dappling the gravel driveway in patches of gold. The sizzle of burgers on the grill and the sound of laughter from the backyard rippled across the open space.

Emily and I had built a home on a few acres at the edge of town, just a couple of miles from the farm I'd grown up on right outside Old Bridge. My brother, Jack, owned it now, running it with his wife and three kids. Emily and Marie had become good friends, but I loved how tight my woman was with the other Iron Rogues' old ladies. It only knitted our family even closer.

I was crouched beside a sleek black-and-red go-kart parked just in front of the garage, one knee on the warm pavement, both hands steady as I buckled in the most important driver I'd ever trained. My son, Archer—four years old today—was already bouncing in his seat, legs too short to reach the pedals without the custom rig Axle built last week. The kid looked like he was ready to win the Daytona 500.

"Steering tight?" I asked, tugging the straps snug across his chest. His Iron Rogues ball cap sat backward on his head, and a streak of chocolate cake still smudged the corner of his mouth.

He gave a serious nod, biting his bottom lip the way he did when he concentrated. "Ready to ride, Daddy."

"Alright then," Axle said, wiping his hands on a shop towel. "Let's fire this thing up."

My brother-in-law had grease under his fingernails and his boots planted wide, looking half proud, half exasperated—as though he couldn't believe he was helping a kid who just learned to spell his own name get behind the wheel of a tiny machine capable of hitting forty. If I hadn't added a governor to keep it from going that fast.

Jack came around the corner from the backyard and chuckled. "Just like his dad. You've been riding bikes since you could balance one. And you were racing at what? Fourteen?"

"To his mother's terror," my mom added as she and my dad joined us.

Grinning, I straightened, rolling my shoulders as the engine whirred to life and Archer let out an excited whoop. Before I could step back, I heard it—the soft click of a camera, followed by a voice that spread warmth through my entire body.

"My boys," Emily murmured, barefoot on the driveway as she held our one-year-old daughter, River, on her hip, snapping a photo with her phone.

She looked like summer herself with her long blond hair braided over one shoulder, white cotton sundress fluttering around her knees, glowing tanned skin, and that gorgeous smile that filled every dark corner of my life with light. Our little girl rested drowsily against her, cheeks pink from the heat, and her chubby fingers tangled in the lace trim of Emily's dress.

I walked to them with purpose in my step, the space between us vanishing like nothing.

Emily tilted her head back, her lips parting slightly just before I kissed her—slow and soft, savoring her flavor as though I hadn't tasted her in weeks instead of hours. I leaned in to kiss our daughter's head, breathing in her sweet baby scent. Then I wrapped my arms around them both, one hand stroking the dip of Emily's back, the other cradling her waist.

Together, we stood and watched as our son took off, the go-kart zipping down the long stretch of driveway with just enough wobble to make my heart lurch, then steady again.

"This," I said low against Emily's ear, "is what heaven looks like."

She let out a shaky breath, and when I looked down, I saw tears glistening in her eyes.

"Hey," I murmured, brushing my thumb gently beneath her lashes. "What's wrong, angel?"

"I just..." She laughed softly, her smile sheepish, but her voice thick. "He's getting so big, Jude. I swear, I blinked, and he turned four. And next time I blink...he's gonna be sixteen and asking to borrow the Charger."

I snorted, pulling her tighter against me. "Not a chance in hell. He's not touching her till he's got a full beard and a fuc–uh, freaking mortgage."

"Fuh!" our daughter yelled suddenly, tossing her arm toward her brother's go-kart as if she was cheering him on.

Emily gave me the look. "Seriously?"

"I didn't even really say it," I argued, lifting my hands. "Swear to—"

Her eyes narrowed further, and I cut myself off with a cough.

Some of my rougher edges might have smoothed a bit over the years—married life had that effect—but I was still me. And that meant trouble rolled off my tongue before I had time to catch it. My wife just shook her head and kissed our daughter's cheek before heading back toward the house.

I watched them walk away—two pieces of my soul wrapped up in sunshine and a low hum of love that never went away. Then I turned to look at my son again, tearing down the driveway with joy painted all over his face. And for a moment, the whole world went quiet.

There was nothing but contentment. Pure and sweet.

That night, after the sun went down and the grill was cooled, my family—both by blood and oath—all headed out.

Emily and I got the kids to bed, a feat of epic

proportions when they were stimulated from the party and stuffed with sugar. Then we showered off the sweat and barbecue smoke.

I admired her as she stood in the doorway of our bedroom, brushing her hair in slow, sleepy strokes while one of my old club shirts hung loosely off her shoulders, barely skimming her thighs. Her nipples pressed against the thin fabric, her curves soft and tempting in the warm lamplight.

She caught me watching. But then I hadn't bothered to hide it.

Her smile was slow and knowing as she let the brush drop to the dresser before she stepped toward the bed. I reached for her, dragging her onto my lap, one hand slipping under the shirt to cup her bare tit.

"You still sad, baby?" I asked quietly, brushing my thumb over her nipple.

She shivered, and I whipped the shirt off before leaning down to flick it with my tongue. Warm milk beaded at the tip, and I groaned. Fuck, she tasted sweet.

She gasped, rocking her hips over my growing erection.

"Maybe a little," she whispered. "I love watching them grow, but I miss the days when he was tiny."

I wrapped an arm around her waist, dragging her under me as I leaned her back onto the bed.

"Then let's make another one," I suggested, my voice rough and my cock already throbbing against her belly. We both wanted a big family, so I knew it wouldn't take much convincing, if any, for her to agree.

She moaned, arching into me. "Really?"

"Hell, yes. I want to fill this house with the sound of little feet and giggles."

Emily sighed dreamily. "You mean it?"

"Angel, I've been meaning it since the moment you gave me our son." I bent to suck at her other nipple, drinking her sweet cream and savoring the way her fingers tangled in my hair. "Every time I see you swollen with my baby, I swear I fall in love all over again."

"Jude..."

"It's sexy as fuck, baby. Especially when your tits are swollen and dripping." I caressed her flat belly and murmured, "Want you full of my kid, round and glowing. Want everyone who sees you to know who you belong to."

She grinned through a breathless laugh. "Admit it, you enjoy showing me off. Like some kind of caveman proving his virility."

"That too." I grinned as I nudged her thighs apart. "And we make damn cute kids."

What followed was slow and filthy, a promise in every thrust, devotion in every kiss.

"Gonna breed you, angel," I growled when my spine began to tingle and her pussy tightened, ready to climax. "Come, baby. Want you to take every drop."

Emily grabbed a pillow and shoved it over her face right before she screamed. Her muscles rippled around my cock and milked me until I filled her with my seed, groaning her name and whispering how she was mine—always.

I collapsed on top of her, our heartbeats racing and panting as we tried to catch our breath.

"Mamamama!" Our daughter's voice crackled through the baby monitor.

I dropped my head to the valley between her tits and sighed. "These little cockblockers."

Emily giggled, her fingers running through my damp hair. "At least she waited this time."

"Fair point." I kissed the tip of each breast, then her collarbone, and finally her throat. "Still want another one?"

"Are you sure you do?" she teased, voice sweet and lazy.

I flexed my cock inside her, making her gasp. "Hell yes. Seeing you pregnant is the hottest damn thing on earth."

Her smile turned wicked. "You just like the way people look at me when I'm carrying your baby. So it's stamped all over me that I'm yours."

"It is." I kissed her hard. "But I like the truth of it, too. You're mine. Forever."

"Mamamama!" River shouted again, sounding a little put out this time.

Emily giggled happily as I rolled off the bed, tugging on a pair of sweatpants.

"Get some rest," I told her, brushing a lock of hair off her flushed face. "Gonna go take care of my baby girl. Then I'm coming back to make another one."

A shiver ran through her, and her eyes heated, the blue turning to sapphire.

Before I left, I leaned down, kissed her softly, and murmured, "I love you, angel."

She smiled brightly, as though it was the first time I'd ever said it. Maybe in some way, it always was. Every time I said those words, they meant more than the last.

Because with Emily, everything only got better.

And I was never letting go.

If you're curious about Kane, there's good news! His book will be first in the new Redline Kings MC series!

And if you join our newsletter, you'll get a FREE copy of The Virgin's Guardian, which was banned on Amazon.

## ABOUT THE AUTHOR

The writing duo of Elle Christensen and Rochelle Paige team up under the Fiona Davenport pen name to bring you sexy, insta-love stories filled with alpha males. If you want a quick & dirty read with a guaranteed happily ever after, then give Fiona Davenport a try!

[Instagram] [TikTok] [BB] [Facebook]

Printed in Dunstable, United Kingdom